JUSTICE

Terrorists don't care who they kill or hurt; they're not interested in justice for other people, only in bombs and guns and killing – and in escaping from the law themselves. But there is another kind of justice, an older kind, before there were police and laws and prisons. It's called an eye for an eye, a tooth for a tooth, a life for a life . . .

The bomb goes off in the Queen's coach outside Parliament, killing five people, and only just missing the Queen. Jane Cole is watching from the crowd. Her father was driving the Queen's coach, and now Jane, sick with fear, pushes through the terrified crowd to look for him. She finds him lying on the ground, covered in blood and screaming in pain.

Alan Cole lives, but he loses his leg. And the terror for him and his daughter is only just beginning, because Alan knows something about the terrorists. He hasn't realized it yet, but he soon will.

And somebody, somewhere, desperately wants to stop Alan Cole realizing . . . and talking.

OXFORD BOOKWORMS LIBRARY
Thriller & Adventure

Justice

Stage 3 (1000 headwords)

Series Editor: Jennifer Bassett
Founder Editor: Tricia Hedge
Activities Editors: Jennifer Bassett and Christine Lindop

TIM VICARY

Justice

OXFORD UNIVERSITY PRESS

OXFORD

UNIVERSITY PRESS

Great Clarendon Street, Oxford OX2 6DP

Oxford University Press is a department of the University of Oxford.
It furthers the University's objective of excellence in research, scholarship,
and education by publishing worldwide in

Oxford New York

Auckland Cape Town Dar es Salaam Hong Kong Karachi
Kuala Lumpur Madrid Melbourne Mexico City Nairobi
New Delhi Shanghai Taipei Toronto

With offices in

Argentina Austria Brazil Chile Czech Republic France Greece
Guatemala Hungary Italy Japan Poland Portugal Singapore
South Korea Switzerland Thailand Turkey Ukraine Vietnam

OXFORD and OXFORD ENGLISH are registered trade marks of
Oxford University Press in the UK and in certain other countries

ISBN 978 0 19 479119 9

Typeset by Wyvern Typesetting Ltd, Bristol

Printed in China

ACKNOWLEDGEMENTS
Illustrated by: Adam Willis/Artist Partners Ltd

Word count (main text): 10,420 words

For more information on the Oxford Bookworms Library,
visit www.oup.com/bookworms

CONTENTS

1
BOMB

'Look!' Jane Cole said. 'Here she comes now!'

The two Americans looked along the street. There were crowds of people everywhere. In the middle of the road, soldiers were riding towards them on horseback. Behind them came a golden coach, pulled by six black horses.

'That's my father,' Jane said. 'He's the coachman – the man driving the horses.'

The American woman said: 'Fantastic! Your father's driving the Queen! Quick, Harry, use the video camera!'

'I *am* using it!' her husband said. 'But she's too far away. Can't we get a little nearer, Jane?'

'We can try,' Jane said. 'Follow me!' She took them nearer to the entrance to Parliament. 'This is where the coach will stop and the Queen will get out. Then she'll go upstairs to open Parliament for this year.'

'Didn't someone put a bomb under your Parliament once?' the American man asked. 'I read about that at school. Guy . . . something?'

'Guy Fawkes,' Jane said. 'In 1605. He tried to blow up Parliament, that's right. But don't worry. There's no Guy Fawkes here today.'

She smiled at the Americans. She was a student, and this was her part-time job – to show tourists round London.

1

She felt proud to show them her father, driving the Queen on a wonderful day like this.

Then the Queen's coach came past in front of them, the golden roof bright in the sunlight.

There were people everywhere, trying to take photos. Jane saw a woman with red-brown hair behind the American man, pressing the button of her camera. That's stupid, Jane thought; she can only see the backs of people's heads there. The woman shook her camera angrily; there seemed to be something wrong with it. The American woman pulled Jane forward, laughing happily. 'Come on,' she said, 'let's get to the front! Use that video, Harry!'

Alan Cole stopped the coach outside Parliament, and sat there, quietly holding the horses. A man opened the coach door, and Prince Charles and the Duke of Edinburgh got out. Then the Queen got out. She was wearing a long white dress, and carrying a gold handbag. She walked slowly towards the entrance to the building.

'Excuse me, please,' the woman with red-brown hair said. 'I must get closer.' She pushed past Jane and held out her small black camera.

'Oh, all right,' Jane said. 'But . . . *my God!*'

There was a loud BANG! Jane saw a bright white light in front of her eyes, and felt a terrible hot wind on her face. The wind threw her backwards, and she fell to the ground with a lot of other people. For a moment she lay there, not thinking, not seeing.

Her eyes were open but she saw nothing. Only . . . blue

The woman shook her camera angrily.

sky. She heard nothing. Only . . . silence. Her body felt no pain. But she could smell something. Smoke.

Smoke? she thought. I don't understand. Why smoke? And this blue sky. Where am I?

Then the screaming began.

The screaming was high and loud and terrible. It didn't sound human. It went on and on and on.

Jane saw a hand in front of her, on the ground. A man's hand with blood on it. And broken glass. She moved her head and saw broken glass everywhere, and blood, and bodies lying on the ground. She stood up slowly.

For a moment she thought everyone was dead. There were bodies everywhere, but no one was moving. Then a man ran across the road, and one of the bodies moved.

The body wasn't human; it was a horse. As it moved, it screamed. The horse tried to stand up, but it couldn't, because it only had three legs. There was blood all round the horse, and a big bit of wood in its stomach.

The Queen's coach was broken into a thousand pieces, and there were bits of wood and clothes and bodies everywhere. The bodies looked like broken dolls.

'Dad!' she screamed. 'Oh God – *my father*!'

She ran quickly towards the coach. A policeman with a bloody hand tried to stop her, but she pushed him away.

'My father's over there!' she screamed.

At first she couldn't find him. There were so many bodies – and so much blood! She saw the horse in the middle of a great lake of blood, trying to get up on its front leg. There was blood coming from the horse's nose and stomach – and under the back legs, something that looked like . . .

A body. A man. '*Father!*'

Alan Cole was covered with blood and his face was as white as paper. When he saw Jane, he opened his eyes and screamed. 'It's my leg! My leg – get this horse off me!'

His leg was under the back of the horse, which was moving wildly, trying to get up. Each time the horse moved, it fell on Alan Cole's leg, and he screamed.

Jane ran and pushed the horse but it was too big, too heavy. She pulled its tail but that was no good. It tried to get up and fell on her father's leg again, twice. She could hear his bones breaking. Then a policeman came and held the horse's leg. Jane held its tail, and another policeman held Alan's arms. Jane and the first policeman pulled the horse to one side, while the second policeman pulled Alan free. The horse screamed, kicked Jane on the shoulder, and died.

• • •

Jane went in the ambulance with her father to the hospital. There were lots of people there. She heard a reporter talking on the telephone to his office.

'Five,' he said. 'Five dead, and about thirty are very badly hurt. It was a bomb – it must be terrorists. But the Queen is safe. She was inside Parliament with her husband and Prince Charles and . . .'

'Never mind the bloody Queen!' Jane thought. 'What about my father!'

The doctors took Alan away from Jane, and she had to

'Get this horse off me!'

sit and wait. Her shoulder was hurt, but not badly. For nearly four hours she walked up and down, drank coffee, and thought: *why?*

Why try to kill the Queen – how will that help anyone? Why kill tourists and soldiers outside Parliament? *Why try to kill my father?*

Jane's father was the most important person in the world to her. When he was a soldier, she had travelled around the world with him. He had taught her to climb mountains, win judo fights, ride horses, sail boats – he was a great father. Now, she thought, he may be dead.

At midnight, a young Indian doctor came to see her. He was tired and serious. He looked at her sadly.

'It's bad news, isn't it?' Jane said. 'Is he dead?'

'No, Miss Cole,' the doctor said. 'We have saved your father's life. But I am afraid . . .' He hesitated.

'Yes? What then? Please – tell me!'

'I am afraid he has lost his leg. It was too badly broken – we had to cut it off.'

'Oh my God!' Jane sat down suddenly. 'You cut his leg off!' She stared at the doctor and thought: Dad will never be able to climb or ride or sail again. Oh, poor man! It's worse than being dead! She began to cry.

'I'm very sorry, miss,' the doctor said. 'We had to do it, to save his life. He'll get an artificial leg. He'll learn to use it. At least he's alive . . .'

'Yes, I suppose so.' Jane looked up. 'I'm sorry, doctor. I'm sure you did your best. Can I see him now?'

'Yes, of course. The nurse will show you . . .'

In the hospital bed, Alan Cole lay quietly. His face was as white as the sheets on the bed, but when Jane came in, he opened his eyes slowly. Jane took one of his hands in hers. The hand was cold, like ice.

'Janie? Are you all right?'

'Me? I'm fine, Dad. And you're going to be OK too, aren't you? The doctor told me.'

He closed his eyes, and for a long time he didn't answer. Perhaps he's asleep again, Jane thought. Then, very quietly, Alan Cole said: 'Stay with me, Janie.'

'Of course, Dad. I'm not going anywhere.' Jane sat down on a chair beside the bed. 'You sleep now.'

Her father closed his eyes, and the nurse smiled at Jane. 'Would you like a cup of tea, miss?'

'Yes, please,' Jane said. 'It's going to be a long night.' She held her father's hand, and watched him sleeping. He looks happy now, she thought. Like a baby.

But what will he say when I tell him about the leg?

• • •

Next day, the doctor told Alan about his leg. Jane sat by the bed and held his hand while he listened. He didn't say anything, but tears came into his eyes.

'I'm very sorry, Mr Cole,' the doctor said. 'But we had to do it. Your leg was broken in forty places, and you lost a lot of blood. You're lucky to be alive.'

'Lucky!' Alan Cole said angrily. 'With this? Damn it, man, I'll never walk again!'

'Oh yes, you will, Mr Cole. We'll get you an artificial leg. They're very good – they move like an ordinary leg. No one will see it under your trousers.'

'And will I be able to ride horses with it, or swim, or climb mountains?'

'Well, perhaps not . . .' The doctor hesitated. 'We'll do our best for you, Mr Cole, believe me. Now, here's something to help you sleep. You'll feel better later.'

All day, Jane waited in the hospital. She drank tea, read newspapers, had a meal, and held her father's hand as he slept. No one came to visit. Her mother was dead, and her brother lived in Australia. At four o'clock her father woke up, and looked at her with big frightened eyes.

'Janie?' he said.

'Yes, Dad.'

'What happened? The doctor said there was a bomb, didn't he? And I lost my leg. But . . . I can't remember.'

Very quietly, Jane told him what she had seen. Then she read the newspaper aloud.

Five people have died, and forty are in hospital. One man from the Queen's coach lost a leg, and the other three are dead. But the Queen, Prince Charles, and the Duke of Edinburgh were not hurt. Yesterday some Irish terrorists rang the BBC to say they exploded the bomb. 'We are sorry that ordinary people died,' they said. 'We meant to kill the Queen, not them. But accidents happen sometimes. The Queen was lucky this time, because the bomb exploded

Jane stroked her father's hand softly.

too late. But *she* has to be lucky every time. *We* only
have to be lucky once.'

'My God!' Alan said. 'The bastards! Who . . . who died?'

'One policeman, a tourist, and three coachmen,' Jane said.
'You were the only coachman who didn't die.'

'Oh no.' Alan's eyes filled with tears. 'George, Bernard,
John – dead! What harm had they ever done to the Irish, or
to anyone? Why did the Irish have to kill *them* with their
bloody bomb? There's no justice in this life, is there?'

'Well, perhaps the police will . . .' Jane began.

'Yes, I hope they catch those murdering Irish bastards, I
really do. I hope they lock them in prison until they die. That's
what I hope. By God, I do!'

'Of course they will, Dad.' Jane stroked her father's
hand softly. 'The police are out there now, looking for the
bombers. They'll catch them, before too long.'

2

Anna

That night Alan was moved to another hospital, where they
would fit him with an artificial leg. Jane went with him and
slept in a visitor's room there. In the morning she bought a
newspaper. She was right about the police. 'They've got
them, Dad!' she said. 'Read this!'

Police yesterday arrested two Irishmen who they think

put a bomb in the Queen's coach last week. The police said: 'Last week the coach went to a factory in south London to have new wheels fitted, and we believe the bomb was placed in the coach there. The two Irishmen worked at this factory, and two days before the bombing, they went on holiday to Ireland. We think the bomb had a clock in it, which was meant to explode at eleven o'clock outside Parliament. Luckily for the Queen, the bomb exploded after she had left the coach.'

Alan Cole put the newspaper down slowly. He looked pleased. 'Thank God for that,' he said.

'But why did they want the bomb to explode outside Parliament?' Jane asked. 'The Queen was in the coach for twenty minutes – why not blow the coach up earlier?'

'I don't know. Perhaps they wanted good pictures on TV,' Alan said. 'It was lucky for the Queen. But not lucky for me, or for the poor people who were killed.'

'No.' Jane put her hand on her father's, and remembered those minutes outside Parliament. The American man using his video camera, and the woman with red-brown hair shaking her camera angrily. Then . . . she shut her eyes, and saw the smoke, and the horse screaming, and the blood and bodies everywhere . . .

What kind of people could do that?

'I suppose the terrorists watched it on TV,' she said. 'They were in Ireland when the bomb exploded.'

'I expect they did,' Alan said. 'I expect they were laughing as people died. But I'm pleased the police have caught them. Now perhaps they'll leave me alone.'

'Who? The police? Dad, what do you mean?'

Alan sighed. 'Well, yesterday they came to ask me about the night before the bombing. I went back to the Mews at about ten o'clock that night, you know, to look at a horse with a bad leg. I often do that. They asked if I saw anything strange, or looked at the coach.'

'And what did you tell them?'

Alan looked angry. 'What do you think, Jane? Of course I saw nothing strange! I was looking at the horse, not the coach. And we were only there half an hour.'

'*We*, Dad?' Jane asked. 'Was someone with you?'

Alan hesitated. 'Well, yes . . . a lady friend of mine, Anna. You haven't met her, Jane, but I've told her about you. She's nice, you'll like her. She sometimes comes to see the horses with me.'

Jane felt embarrassed. After her mother had died four years ago, Jane had lived at home with her father. Once, he had brought a woman home to the house, but Jane had had a terrible argument with her, and the woman had left. There had been no other women, until Jane left home to go to university. Now . . .?

Well, her father was an adult, of course he could have women friends. But Jane hated it. She had loved her mother too much. And she loved her father too.

'What kind of a woman is she?' she asked angrily.

He's *my* father, she thought – I don't want another woman

13

taking him away from me.

'Tall. Pretty. Red-brown hair. She likes horses and . . . films. We go to the cinema a lot.'

'Is she in love with you?'

'Well . . . perhaps, Janie, I don't know. I've only known her a few weeks. You'll like her, Janie, she's good fun.'

Jane was still angry, she couldn't stop herself. 'Then why isn't she here? Why hasn't she come to visit you?'

Now Alan looked embarrassed. 'Well, I was going to ask you, Janie . . . she doesn't have a phone, you see, and . . . perhaps she thinks I'm dead, like the others. God knows what she'll think of a man with one leg, but I do want to see her . . . so I've written this letter. Could you post it for me, Janie? Please?'

Jane took the letter and read the address. *Anna Barry, 14 Bowater Gardens, London NE11.*

'Dad, your name was in the newspapers. This woman can read, can't she? She must know you're alive.'

'Yes, but . . . perhaps she doesn't know which hospital. I don't know. Janie, please – don't be difficult.'

'Have you told the police about this woman, Dad?'

'Not yet.'

'Why not? They'll ask her questions, won't they?'

Alan sighed. 'Yes, I suppose so. I warned her about that in the letter. Perhaps that's why she hasn't come. You see . . . it's a bit difficult, Janie. Anna has a husband . . . and so it will be embarrassing for her if he finds out about us. Perhaps the police will want to ask her husband questions, too, and

'It's a bit difficult, Janie. Anna has a husband.'

then there'll be all kinds of trouble.'

'I see,' Jane said. She felt miserable. My own father, she thought, in love with a married woman. Then she saw the tears in his eyes, and his tired white face; and felt angry with herself, not him. Why shouldn't my father fall in love, she thought? It happens to everyone, and you can't always choose the best person. Now he's here with only one leg and I'm angry with him. I'm his daughter, I should help him! Perhaps this Anna really is a nice woman, with a cruel husband.

She smiled, and said: 'I'm sorry, Dad. Of course I'll post your letter. But . . . isn't it a bit dangerous, sending a letter? Her husband could read it.'

'No, it's OK. Bowater Gardens is just where she's living at the moment. It isn't her home. I don't know where her husband lives. I don't want to know.' He smiled and took her hand. 'She's a lovely woman, Janie, really she is. You'll like her if you meet her, you know.'

• • •

Outside the hospital, Jane walked slowly down the street. She felt sad, and a little lonely. I wish my mother was still alive, she thought. I wish Mum was alive now, sitting with Dad in the hospital. I don't want all these problems. Why does Dad need another woman?

Oh Mum, why did you die? I need someone to talk to.

She took the letter out of her pocket and looked at it. I wonder what this Anna Barry is like, she thought. Perhaps she *is* nice, like Dad says. Perhaps I could talk to *her*. Perhaps she really does love Dad; perhaps *she* can help me look after him.

But why hasn't she come to see him?

She looked at the address again. 14 Bowater Gardens, London NE11. That wasn't far from her own student flat.

Why not take the letter myself? she thought. Then, if this Anna opens the door, I can talk to her myself. If I meet her, at least I'll find out what she's like.

Jane put the letter in her bag and walked quickly to the underground station. Am I full of anger, she wondered. Or hope?

• • •

14 Bowater Gardens was an old house in a quiet street in north London. Jane took the letter out of her bag, and rang the bell. Nothing happened.

Damn! she thought. She rang again. Still no answer. She tried the door, but it was locked. So she put the letter through the letter-box and turned away. Then she stopped.

I've come all this way to meet this woman, Jane thought, and I want to know what she's like. She's important to my father so she's important to me. I'll wait.

As she stood there, a woman came out of the house next door. She had grey hair and the kind of face that enjoys watching the neighbours and talking about them.

'They've gone; there's no use waiting,' the woman said. 'I saw you ring the bell so I came to tell you.'

'Are you sure?' Jane said. 'I was looking for Anna.'

'The girl with red hair? That's right, she did live here, but she moved out with her boyfriend two days ago. It was the morning of that terrible bomb – that's why I remember it. The house is empty now. I had a look through the windows,

'They've gone; there's no use waiting.'

and they've taken everything.'

Boyfriend! So Anna had another lover, Jane thought. Not just Dad. My poor, poor father!

'Did you know them well?' the woman asked.

'No, not really,' Jane said. 'I just wanted to . . .'

'They were only here about three months,' the woman went on. 'They weren't very friendly. Never said good morning or anything like that. They were Irish, I think. Well, he was. There's a lot of Irish around here.'

Jane began to move away from the door, and the woman added, helpfully, 'Perhaps your friend will write to you.'

'Yes. Perhaps.' Jane smiled at her and walked sadly down the street.

So that was the kind of woman Anna was. She probably never loved my father at all, Jane thought. How am I going to tell him? Poor Dad! Perhaps I'll just say that I posted the letter, and not tell him that I came to the house and found out about her.

But Jane wasn't very good at lying, and she didn't want to look at her father's sad eyes and tired white face. Let him hope for a few more hours, she thought. I'll go home now and tell him something tomorrow.

She hadn't been back to her flat since the bombing. She loved having her own home. It was only one big bedroom really, with a small bathroom and kitchen. But it was her own place; she could do what she liked there.

She shut the door, then took off her coat and threw it on the bed. Then she heard the bathroom door slowly open behind her. She jumped round, her heart beating fast with fear, and saw a woman standing in the doorway!

'Who the hell are you?' she screamed. A thief, she thought. Jane had learned judo from her father; she knew what to do. She grabbed the woman's arm and threw her towards the bed. But as the woman fell, she grabbed Jane's hair, pulling it forwards, to stop herself from falling. Jane screamed, and pushed a hand into the woman's face, harder and harder until her hair was free. Then she hit the woman in the face and she fell to the floor. Jane stepped back, looked at her, and saw . . .

A man coming out of the kitchen. He had cold grey eyes and a thin hard smile and worst of all he had a gun in his hand. He said: 'Don't.'

Jane stood still, shaking. 'Don't what?'

'Move. Or talk. Don't do anything.' The little black hole in the end of the gun watched her, like a cold eye.

The woman got up off the floor, pulled Jane onto a chair, and tied her hands behind her. Then Jane remembered that there were people in the other flats, and opened her mouth to scream. The man hit her in the face.

'Don't even think about it,' he said. He took a long piece of cloth out of his pocket and tied it twice round her head, covering her mouth and the lower part of her face. Jane felt her body shaking with fear. Who were these people? What did they want with her? She stared at the man's cold hard face, the woman's blue eyes and red-brown hair. She thought she had seen the woman before. But where?

Who were these people? What did they want with her?

The woman tied Jane's legs to the chair. The little black eye of the gun was only a few centimetres from her face. The man watched her and smiled. 'Just sit still and be sensible, little girl,' he said. 'Then perhaps you'll live a few hours longer.'

3

'I made him happy'

Alan Cole lay in his bed, listening to a bird singing in the hospital garden. It was nearly dark outside now, and very quiet. He liked to lie like this, remembering.

He remembered the way Anna had kissed him, and looked into his eyes. He remembered her red-brown hair, her blue eyes, the soft, dry touch of her lips, her deep, happy laugh. She liked to drink whisky before they made love, and afterwards, she often held his head on her chest and stroked his hair.

I loved that, he remembered. I felt like a child again, safe and comfortable. Sometimes I fell asleep.

And then what? On the night before the bombing, he and Anna had been out for a meal in a restaurant. Then they had gone to the Mews to look at the horses. The guards knew she was his girlfriend, so they didn't think it was unusual. One of the horses, Sandman, had hurt his leg that morning, Alan remembered. In the evening the leg had been hot, so he had put ice on it. Lucky Sandman, he thought – he couldn't pull

They had gone to the Mews to look at the horses.

the coach next day, so he was still alive now.

Afterwards they went back to his house and made love. Anna had been very excited, Alan remembered; it had been very good. Then he had slept until morning. He woke at six o'clock and dressed quietly, but she woke up just before he left. She opened her eyes, smiled at him, and held out her arms to him sleepily. He kissed her, and she said: 'Goodbye, lover.'

That was the last time he had seen her.

He was still thinking about Anna when he drove the Queen's coach to Parliament, with the six fine horses in front of him. For a moment he thought he saw her in the crowd, watching . . .

Alan didn't want to think about what had happened next. He stared into the darkness outside the hospital window and thought: why hasn't she come to see me?

Perhaps she never really loved me, he thought. Perhaps she's gone back to her husband, or found a younger man. It's cruel and painful, but I can't change it. I'll never see her again.

He remembered her warm body next to his, and the way she whispered his name. There must be another reason. She loves me, I know she does. She'll come to see me when she gets my letter.

I wish Jane could meet her.

Outside, night had fallen, and the birds had stopped singing. Alan Cole lay quietly on his bed, the tears running slowly down his face.

• • •

Jane sat on the chair in her flat and listened to the man and woman arguing in her kitchen. She could hear, but she couldn't speak or see, because the man had put a bag over her head. Her arms and legs were still tied to the chair, and her face ached where the man had hit her.

She tried to get her hands free. She pulled as hard as she could, but the rope just burned her wrists. All she could do was listen to the voices in the kitchen.

'We must phone him *now*, Kev. We can't wait.'

'We've got to wait. It's too dangerous to do it from here, Anna. Wait until we're ready to go.'

Anna! Jane thought. Was this her father's Anna? No, no, lots of women were called Anna.

'But we can't go until tonight,' Anna said. 'There are too many people around during the day. And every minute is important! Perhaps Cole has already talked to the police about me. Oh God, I wish the bomb had killed him with the others!'

'Well, it didn't. And it didn't kill the Queen.'

Jane's body was shaking. This *was* her father's Anna! She was talking about her father, and the bomb. And then Jane remembered where she had seen the woman before.

Outside Parliament, with a camera, shaking it angrily. Taking photos of the back of people's heads. Then pushing forwards to get closer, pressing the camera button again . . . a second before the bomb exploded.

The voices in the kitchen stopped. The door opened,

someone came into the room. *What now?*

Jane heard the click of a gun.

• • •

'Phone call for you, Mr Cole. You're popular today, aren't you?' The nurse smiled, pushed the telephone table next to his bed, and went out.

Alan picked up the phone. 'Hello?'

'Mr Cole? This is Detective David Hall. You remember I came to see you yesterday. I'm ringing because I've got a few more questions to ask you. Is it all right if I come over to see you now?'

'Er . . . well, I suppose so. But I've told you everything I know.'

'Yes, I'm sure. But it's just that we have to get all the facts right. I'll come over now, if that's OK?'

'Yes, fine. I . . .'

'Great! See you in a few minutes, then.'

Alan put the phone down slowly. He felt old, and tired, and very, very lonely. Perhaps I'll ring Jane later when this man's gone, he thought. I hope she remembered to post the letter.

• • •

Kev pulled the bag off Jane's head and she saw the gun a few centimetres from her eyes. 'I'm going to untie this cloth round your mouth,' Kev said. 'If you scream, I'll put a bullet through your head. This gun is silenced, no one will hear anything.'

They untied the cloth and pulled her chair over to the

wall, where the phone was. The gun was pointing at her head all the time.

'Do just what we tell you,' Anna said. 'And everything will be all right.'

Jane was suddenly wild with anger. She said: 'You're Anna, aren't you? My father loves you – he thinks you're wonderful. But you don't care about him at all, do you? You wish the bomb had killed him.'

'Of course I care about him,' Anna said softly. 'He's very important to me. That's why I'm going to phone him now, and you're going to talk to him too.'

Jane stared at her, then at Kev. 'Why?'

Anna laughed. 'I'm going to ask him to keep our love a secret. I have a very difficult husband, you know.'

What's the woman talking about? Jane thought. What does all this mean? Then, suddenly, a lot of things came together in her mind, and everything became clear. Anna had been with her father in the Mews on the night before the bombing. In the kitchen Anna had spoken about her father talking to the *police*. Jane could hear from Kev's voice that he was Irish, and he and Anna had moved out of Bowater Gardens on the morning of the bombing. Later, Anna had been outside Parliament, doing strange things with a camera when the bomb exploded. If it *was* a camera. Perhaps it had been a radio, sending a signal to the bomb. *Oh God!*

'You're the terrorists, aren't you?' she whispered. '*You* did it, Anna. *You* put the bomb in the Queen's coach. You exploded it with a camera. I saw you, outside Parliament.

You're terrorists – murdering terrorists, both of you!'

Kev smiled coldly. 'Well, well. What a clever little girl! But you're wrong. The police have arrested the terrorists. It was in the newspapers this morning.'

'You're the terrorists, aren't you?' Jane whispered.

'So? They're the wrong men, aren't they? It was you two, I know it was! You killed five people, and took away my father's leg, and now two innocent men will go to prison for thirty years, for something *you* did. But you don't care.'

Kev's eyes were suddenly full of hate. 'Care? About what? We're fighting to free Ireland. If the British put the wrong people in prison, that's not our problem. We care about staying free. That's good for Ireland.'

'Yes, and I suppose it's good for Ireland to use innocent people like my father – to make love to him just because you wanted to get into the Mews to put the bomb in the coach. Did you enjoy that, Anna? Do you feel proud of it?'

Anna laughed, a strange, quiet, cruel laugh. 'Yes, of course I enjoyed it, little girl. And your father enjoyed it too. I made him happy.'

'Happy!' Jane said. 'You nearly killed him!'

'Yes. I'm sorry he didn't die, while he was so happy.'

Silence. There was no answer to that, Jane thought.

'Let's get on with it,' said Kev angrily. 'We're losing time.'

Tears came into Jane's eyes. 'You dirty murderers,' she whispered.

Kev hit her across the face with his gun. Jane felt blood in her mouth. One of her teeth was broken.

'We could kill her now,' Kev said, 'and get out of the country tonight.'

'No, no,' Anna said. 'We must talk to Cole first.'

'But we can't let her go,' Kev said. 'She's seen our faces. She knows too much.'

29

'Oh no,' Anna said. Her voice was soft and cruel. 'Of course not. But we'll keep her alive for some weeks, to make sure that Cole stays quiet. Pick up the phone, Kev.'

4

Phone call

The phone rang again in Alan Cole's room.

'Hello?' he said.

'Alan?'

He recognized her voice at once. 'Anna!' he said, his heart beating fast.

'Yes. Now listen carefully, Alan—'

'Oh Anna! I've been waiting for your call. Have you heard about – about my leg, Anna?'

'Never mind your leg. Listen to me. I'll say this once and once only.'

'What? Anna, what are you—'

'We've got your daughter, Alan. Jane. That's her name, isn't it? Speak to your father, Jane. *Now!*'

Over the phone, Alan heard the high, frightened voice of his daughter. 'Dad? I'm sorry, Dad. They say if you tell the police anything about Anna, they'll kill me, but I don't care, I . . . oh!'

Alan heard a scream, which was suddenly cut off. Then Anna's voice again: 'She won't die if you keep quiet, lover boy. But if you say a word, a single word about me to the police, you'll find her body in the river Thames. Do you understand?'

Alan tried to speak, but there was something wrong with his voice. 'Yes,' he said. 'But, please . . .'

'No buts. If you want to see your daughter again, keep your mouth *shut*.'

The phone went dead. Alan Cole sat very still. There was a terrible pain in his chest, his mouth was dry and he couldn't move. He sat like a stone.

It's like a dream, he thought. Surely it didn't happen. But that voice on the phone, it was Jane all right. And Anna, too. *Anna!* . . . saying that she had kidnapped Jane.

But why? What was going on?

Slowly, he tried to understand. He hadn't told the police about Anna, because of her husband. But why was that so important?

Why has Anna kidnapped Jane?

Because Anna has a secret. Something very important that I, Alan, know about, but mustn't tell the police. Anna will kill Jane if I tell anyone about it.

But what is this secret! What am I supposed to know?

There was a knock on the door. A nurse came in.

'Hello, Mr Cole. A policeman to see you. Are you OK?'

'Yes . . . yes, fine thanks.'

'You don't look OK.' The nurse put her hand on his head, and felt his wrist. 'Well, you're not too hot, and your heart's OK.' She smiled at the policeman. 'Just half an hour, now. Remember, he's had a very serious accident.'

'Remember, he's had a very serious accident.'

'I know that.' The policeman came in and sat down, and the nurse went out, pushing the telephone table in front of her. 'I'm Detective Hall, Mr Cole. We met before.'

'Yes,' Alan said. The policeman had a kind, friendly face. The kind of man you could trust. He'll help me, Alan thought. He's probably a father himself.

No! Fear burned Alan like a fire. *I mustn't tell him about Anna. If I do, Jane will die . . .*

'You've probably read in the newspapers, Mr Cole, that we've arrested two men.' The policeman told Alan the story about the two Irishmen in the coach factory. 'So we know they bombed the coach, and how they did it. I suppose you're pleased about that.'

'Er . . . yes,' Alan said quietly. 'That's good. But . . . why have you come to see me?'

'I just need to ask you a few questions about the day before the bombing. You see, we think these men put the bomb in the coach three days before the bombing, while the coach was at the factory. So the bomb was already in the coach when it came back to the Mews.'

'Was it?' Alan said. He didn't really understand what the policeman was talking about.

'We think so, yes. And in your job, you look after the coach, don't you?'

'The coach, yes. And the horses. Mostly the horses.'

'Well, did you notice anything unusual – anything at all?'

'No, I don't think so.'

'Let's take this slowly,' the policeman said. 'The day before the bombing, when did you leave work?'

'At . . . about six o'clock. Half past, perhaps.'

'And you didn't go back?'

'No,' Alan said quietly.

Then he looked away, quickly, out of the window. He felt cold, frightened, lonely.

'Are you sure about that, Mr Cole? You see, a guard told me you came back later, at about ten.'

'He did? Oh, yes, of course. I went back to see a horse, Sandman. He had a bad leg.'

'I see.' The policeman wrote in his book. 'Alone?'

'I'm sorry?'

'Were you alone, Mr Cole? When you saw the horse?'

For a moment Alan didn't answer. A new, very unwelcome idea came to him, and he began to feel sick with fear. *It wasn't those two Irishmen*, he thought, *it was Anna!* She put the bomb in the coach when I was with Sandman. I was alone with the horse for at least ten minutes; she had plenty of time.

And that means she didn't love me at all, she just used me. I thought I was so lucky, an old man with a young pretty woman in my bed – and all the time she was laughing at me. Worse than that – she's a murderer! She killed George and Bernard and John, and she took my leg, and now she's going to kill Jane as well!

And I can't say anything about it.

That's why she phoned me. To make sure that I never tell the police.

If I tell this policeman, Jane will die.

34

In a strange, shaky voice, Alan said: 'I was alone when I was with the horse, yes.'

The policeman said nothing. Alan felt his hands shaking and put them under the sheet. Why is he looking at me like that? he thought. What does he know?

'Are you sure, Mr Cole? The guard says you have a lady friend, and sometimes she visits the horses with you. Was she with you that night?'

'No.'

'You're sure about that, Mr Cole?'

'Yes, I am. And she's not my friend any more now – we've ended it.'

'I see.' The policeman sighed, wrote in his notebook, and stood up. 'That's all then, Mr Cole. The guard wasn't sure. Probably it was a different night.'

'Yes. I'm sure it was.'

'Right then. Thank you for your help. Goodnight, Mr Cole.' He walked to the door, and went out.

Alan watched him go, unable to say another word. He had never felt so helpless, so frightened. I have to speak, he thought, I have to do something. But I can't.

If I speak, Jane will die.

But if I say nothing, will they ever let her go?

As the door closed, he opened his mouth and said: 'Detective Hall.'

But the policeman walked away. He didn't hear.

Oh God, Alan thought. *What do I do now?*

• • •

After the phone call Kev and Anna tied the cloth round Jane's mouth again, and went back into her kitchen. She had the bag over her head too, but she could hear most of what they were saying. They were angry, arguing.

'You've made too many mistakes with this plan, Anna,'

Jane could hear what they were saying.

Kev said. 'The Queen of England is still walking around Buckingham Palace because of you.'

Anna's voice was high and angry. 'Because of *me*? What about *you*? You're supposed to understand bombs and radio transmitters, and what happens? The transmitter in that camera didn't work when I pressed the button!'

'You probably didn't press it hard enough,' Kev said coldly. 'It worked in the end, didn't it?'

'Yes, too late!' Anna said. 'That was *your* mistake, not mine. So now we've got Cole to worry about, and this girl. We've got to get her away from here fast.'

'Wait until midnight, when the house is quiet.'

There was an icy fear in Jane's stomach. They know I can hear them, and they don't care, she thought. I'm sure Dad will keep quiet, but they can never let me go now. They'll have to kill me, because I know too much.

If I don't get away from them soon, I'm going to die.

• • •

Alan lay in the dark and listened to the voices in his head, arguing this way, and that way, until he thought he would go crazy.

Keep your mouth shut! If you speak, she'll die.

But they'll still kill her, if she's seen their faces.

They won't, Anna won't. She's a woman, she couldn't do that! She was your lover!

Woman! She killed five people! She blew my leg off!

Those two men the police have arrested are innocent. They'll go to prison for thirty years if I don't speak!

I don't know them, I don't care about them. Jane is the only person who matters to me!

The police will think that I helped Anna put the bomb in the coach! I'll go to prison.

That woman is laughing at me. She was laughing at me when we made love. I hate her! I hope she dies!

She won't die, Jane will. I must keep quiet!

What can I do? If I speak, they'll kill her. But if I don't speak, they'll kill her later. So I've got to tell the police now, it's Jane's only chance.

I can't, it's too dangerous. I can't! I want to see my daughter!

For two hours he lay in his room and listened to the voices in his head and thought he was going crazy. His leg ached, his chest felt very hot. Twice he decided to get up and tell someone, but his body wouldn't move.

Then, the third time, he got into his wheelchair and went out into the corridor. It was midnight.

'Nurse!' he said. 'Nurse, I need a telephone, now!'

Oh God, he thought. *Where is Jane now?*

• • •

Jane was in the boot of a car. Her hands and feet were tied, the piece of cloth was round her mouth, and the bag was over her head, but she knew she was in a car boot because she could hear the engine, and when she tried to sit up she hit her head.

She didn't know how long she had been there. There wasn't much air, but she couldn't do anything about it. She just lay there and thought: it can't be much longer. We must get there soon and then they'll let me out.

And then what? How long before they kill me?

5

'You must believe me!'

When Alan phoned the police, Detective Hall came to the hospital quickly, bringing an Inspector Lee with him. They listened to Alan's story, then talked for a while outside the door. Then they came back in.

'OK, Mr Cole,' Inspector Lee said. 'Detectives are now searching the house in Bowater Gardens and your daughter's flat. I've informed the police at ports and airports too. It's possible that the kidnappers will try to take your daughter out of the country, you know.'

'Oh my God.' Alan held his face in his hands. 'She's probably dead. I'll never see her again.'

'Let's hope that's not true,' said the Inspector. 'Now, let's talk about this woman Anna again. Why do you think she's a terrorist?'

Again, Alan explained. The visit to the Mews the evening before the bombing; the ten minutes when Anna was not with him; her phone call, telling him not to talk to the police or Jane would die. It was hard to speak clearly because he was so angry and afraid. He began to cry. 'It's no good,' he said. 'Jane's going to die.'

39

'It's no good,' Alan said. 'Jane's going to die.'

'Try to keep calm, Mr Cole,' said the Inspector. 'You see, we're not sure that this Anna *is* a terrorist. We have already arrested the two men who put the bomb in the coach. In fact, one of them confessed to it this morning. The other one will confess soon.'

'But they're the wrong people – they must be! If *they* are the murderers, why did Anna phone me? Why is she saying she'll kill my daughter if I don't keep quiet about *her*?'

'Are you sure it was Anna's voice on the phone?'

'Of course I am! And it was Jane's voice as well! I know my own daughter's voice, don't I?' Alan shouted.

'Mmm,' the Inspector said slowly. 'Now, your daughter. Was she unhappy to hear about Anna, do you think? Sometimes daughters don't like their fathers to have girlfriends, you know. Perhaps she was angry with you.'

'No. Not really. Well, perhaps a bit.'

'I see some very strange things in my job, Mr Cole, and a lot of them are because of family arguments. It's just possible, you see, that your daughter hasn't been kidnapped at all. Perhaps she's angry with you and wants to stop you seeing Anna. Perhaps – I've seen it happen before – she's asked a friend to ring you and pretend to be Anna . . .'

'No!' Alan shouted. 'Jane isn't like that! She was frightened, I could hear it in her voice on the phone. ANNA HAS KIDNAPPED HER! You must believe me!'

At that moment another detective came in and spoke quietly to Inspector Lee, who immediately got up and left the room. When he came back, his face was serious.

'The house in Bowater Gardens is empty,' he told Alan. 'The two people there left on the morning of the bombing. We didn't find anything useful at your daughter's flat – but we did find her handbag with her flat keys in it. It seems strange for her to go out without her keys, doesn't it?'

'Where is she?' Alan whispered. 'Can you find her?'

'If your daughter has been kidnapped, she could be anywhere,' the Inspector said. 'Our only hope is that the kidnappers call you again, and then we can find out where the call came from. We're fixing up a phone for you now, and there'll be two policewomen here with you all night. If Anna does phone, keep her talking. Tell her that you have said nothing to the police, and ask to speak to Jane. Say you must hear her voice.'

They put the phone on a table next to Alan's bed. He stared at it, saying to himself over and over again:

I must hear her voice. I must hear her voice.

• • •

They put Jane in a small bedroom, untied her feet, and took the bag off her head. But they tied her hands behind her back, and then tied them to the end of the bed.

'You'll stay here until those two men are sent to prison,' Anna said. 'Every day we'll send your father a picture of you with today's newspaper, to show you're still alive.'

'Then what?'

'Then . . . we'll see. Perhaps, if your father is a good boy, we'll let you go,' Anna said. 'If you keep quiet too.'

But Jane was watching Kev's face. He won't let me go, she

42

They tied her hands behind her back.

thought. Never. If I don't escape, I'll die here.

When they had left the room, she lay in the dark, wondering how she could escape. I don't want to die, she thought. And how terrible it will be for Dad if they kill me. And then there are those two innocent Irishmen, who will spend thirty years in prison for something they didn't do.

That bastard Kev's going to kill me. I've got to try to escape. I just have to.

For hours she tried to get free but it was impossible. The rope only hurt her wrists more. But at least she could move her hands, up and down the end of the old bed. Once, towards morning, she pulled the rope hard against the bed, but it didn't break. Instead, something cut her hand, and she had an idea.

Could it cut the rope as well?

She moved the rope up and down across the end of the bed. It was very difficult because she couldn't see what she was doing. Three times she cut herself, and there was blood on the rope. But by early morning, the rope broke. Her hands were free! What now?

She tried the door but it was locked. Downstairs, she could hear a radio, and she could smell coffee. So one of them, at least, was in the house.

Then she had another idea. She lay down on the bed and arranged the rope around her wrists, behind her back. Then she screamed: 'Hey! You! Terrorist murderers! Come up here now! I'm thirsty! Get up here and give me a drink!'

In a few minutes, she heard someone on the stairs.

• • •

'Breakfast, Mr Cole,' the nurse said. 'Eat up like a good boy, then you'll feel better.' She smiled.

I'm not a child, Alan thought. Oh God, I'm a father who's lost a child! He pushed the eggs and tomatoes away, and drank a cup of black coffee.

The policewoman in the armchair woke up and smiled brightly. 'Well, no one has phoned, Mr Cole. Perhaps your daughter has been to an all-night party and she'll be along to see you this morning.'

Alan stared at her hopelessly. He had not closed his eyes all night. So the police didn't really believe him. Perhaps they thought he had gone crazy because he had lost a leg. He stared at the silent phone.

Ring, damn you! Ring!

• • •

Kev came in, carrying his cup of coffee in his hand. He wasn't wearing a coat, so Jane could see the gun under his arm. 'Stop making that noise,' he said. 'Or you'll be sorry.'

Jane looked at him. 'You stupid little man,' she said softly, and as Kev stepped angrily forwards, she freed her hands from the rope behind her back and jumped at him. With one hand she pulled his head down, and with the other she grabbed his cup and threw the hot coffee into his face. Then she kicked him hard in the stomach.

'Aaaah! Damn you . . .' Kev fell onto the floor, trying to get the hot coffee out of his eyes. Immediately Jane jumped on top of him. Her knees landed hard in his stomach, and her

She pulled his head down, and threw the hot coffee into his face.

fingers tried to get the gun under his arm. But Kev's hand found the gun first. Jane tried to pull it out of his hand, but he was too strong for her. With his other hand he hit her hard on the side of the head.

Jane fell forwards. But as she fell, she put her head down and bit his nose until her mouth was full of blood. He screamed, tried to pull his head away . . .

And let go of the gun.

I've got it, Jane thought. I've really got it! Then Kev hit her head again, hard, and she didn't know what was happening. She moved away from him, bringing the gun down towards her chest. Her head hurt terribly, and there was blood in her mouth, but all the time her fingers were trying to use the gun.

Why won't it shoot? she thought. How do I make it work? Then as Kev hit her again, there was a BANG and another BANG and a third and a fourth. She didn't know what the bangs were but she held on to the gun as hard as she could and there was a fifth BANG and a sixth . . .

And then it stopped. She opened her eyes and saw that Kev wasn't hitting her any more. His hands had gone all soft and there was blood coming out of his face and his neck and his chest, there was blood all over the floor and half of his head was missing.

Jane stood up, shaking. Where is Anna? she thought.

6

In the tunnel

Alan put down his coffee when the call came. He picked up the phone with shaking hands. A voice said: 'Alan?'

'Anna,' Alan whispered. The policewoman went out of

the door and spoke in a low voice on her radio.

'Do you remember what I said yesterday, Alan?'

'Yes,' Alan said. 'Please don't hurt Jane. Please. I haven't said a word to anyone. I promise you, Anna.'

'Good. Not today, not tomorrow, not ever, Alan. Do you understand? Not if you want her to stay alive.'

'Yes, I understand, Anna. But I must speak to Jane. I must hear her voice, Anna. How do I know you haven't killed her already?' Alan's voice was shaking.

Anna laughed, gently, cruelly. 'We'll send you something, Alan. In a day or two. If you're good.'

'Anna, *please*.'

But the phone went dead.

Alan put the phone down slowly, and suddenly the room was full of voices.

'We've got it! A phone box in South Kensington station, by the ticket office . . .'

'Calling all cars in Kensington, calling all cars in Kensington. A woman has just made a phone call from . . .'

The policewoman put her hand on Alan's arm. 'They'll be there in two minutes,' she said gently. 'They'll—'

'Take me there!' Alan said. 'Please!'

The policewoman looked at him, then at the wheelchair, then back at Alan's white face. 'All right. We've got a big van outside. We can get the wheelchair in that.'

• • •

As Jane came down the stairs, she realized two things; she was covered in blood, and Anna wasn't there.

The house was very quiet, and all the rooms were empty. But I can't go out all covered in blood, she thought. People will think I've killed someone.

I have. But I had to, he was going to kill me. And he's a terrorist. He killed five people, he and Anna . . . I must get out before Anna comes back.

She found a man's coat, put it on, and went out into the street. I should call a policeman, she thought. But she could only see ordinary people, women and children. She saw an underground station and walked towards it.

She went into the station, found some money in the coat pocket, and bought a ticket. I must find my father, she thought, and tell him that everything's all right. Then she looked behind her and saw a woman coming out of a telephone box.

Oh my God, she thought, it's *Anna!*

Jane walked quickly away from the ticket office, down the escalator towards the platform and the trains. Halfway down the escalator she looked back up behind her.

Anna had seen her! She was following her down the escalator!

Quickly, Jane ran down to the bottom and onto one of the platforms. There was a train there, with its doors still open. She ran towards them, but as she ran, the doors closed and the train moved away into the tunnel. Anna was now coming onto the platform behind her. Anna's hand was inside her coat and Jane was sure she had a gun.

Why didn't I bring Kev's gun? Jane thought. But it was

Anna was following her down the escalator!

empty and I hate guns and it's no use thinking about that now. *What do I do now?*

. . .

As the police van screamed through the London traffic, the policewoman listened in to her radio and passed the information to Alan.

'Inspector Lee is on his way,' she said. 'There are six cars at the station already and they're watching all the entrances. Ah! Two detectives have seen a woman with red-brown hair going down the escalator . . .'

'But the trains,' Alan said. 'She'll catch a train . . .'

'They'll stop the trains as soon as they can. But there are hundreds of people in the station. The detectives could lose the woman in the crowds . . .'

'Please God,' whispered Alan. 'Let them catch her.'

. . .

As Anna came towards her, Jane ran towards the end of the platform, then looked behind her and saw Anna running after her, her hand still inside her coat. Quickly, Jane turned and ran towards another escalator, but there was a crowd of people there. She looked again and saw Anna twenty metres behind. She turned round a corner, back onto another platform which was empty – no people, no train. Anna will find me here in a second and shoot me, she thought. *What now?*

She jumped off the platform onto the railway line, and ran into the tunnel.

It was very dark in the tunnel. She knew that one of the

lines was electric. If I touch it, I'll die, she thought. The trains come every six minutes, and if a train hits me, I'll die too. And there are only thirty centimetres between the sides of the train and the tunnel walls.

But there are holes in the tunnel walls every hundred metres, for workmen. I'll find one of those, wait for the next train and then go on to the next hole. It's probably only a kilometre to the next station. And perhaps Anna won't be sure which way I've gone.

She ran on into the darkness. Once she fell, and her hands nearly touched the electric line. When she got up, there was a terrible noise, like a train coming. But it was a train in another tunnel, not this one. She ran on, with one hand on the wall, looking for the hole.

Three minutes, four . . . then she found it! A hole just big enough for one person. She got in and stood very still, waiting. She heard the terrible noise again, this time from the station behind her. Then it stopped. The train will stop in that station for one minute, she thought. Then it will come past.

She laughed aloud in the darkness. Anna is still looking for me back on the platform. How angry she must be!

A hand touched her arm. She screamed. 'What? *Oh God, no!*' The hand grabbed her arm, and pulled her out of the hole, into the dark tunnel.

'Get out there!'

Two hands pushed her and Jane fell between the lines. She got to her knees, carefully, afraid of the electric line. Then the terrible noise started. The ground shook beneath her feet and a white light came towards her, faster and faster. In the light Jane saw Anna standing in the hole, with a gun in her hand. She jumped towards the hole but the train was

Jane saw Anna standing in the hole, with a gun in her hand.

coming faster, much too fast, and there was only room in
the hole for one person, a woman with a gun . . .

• • •

When Alan arrived at the station, there were police cars
everywhere, and crowds of people watching them. The
policewoman helped him out of the van and he pushed his
wheelchair through the crowd, shouting angrily, 'What's
happening? Where is she?'

At the top of the escalator a policeman said: 'I'm sorry,
sir. You can't go down. There's been a terrible accident.'

Then some ambulance men arrived. 'Where is it?' they
asked.

'Down in the tunnel. Two women – a train's hit them,'
the policeman said. The ambulance men hurried down.

'What's happening?' Alan shouted. 'Which women?
There's a murderer down there, a terrorist! And my daughter
– I've got to find my daughter!'

He began to climb out of his wheelchair, but the policeman
pushed him back. 'I'm sorry, sir.'

Then the policewoman hurried up and explained. They
helped Alan's wheelchair onto the escalator and went down.
At the bottom Alan saw an empty train, and a lot of police at
the end of the platform. The ambulance men talked to the
police, and then went into the tunnel. Alan wheeled his chair
slowly along the platform.

Then two of the ambulance men came out of the tunnel.
There was a young woman between them. She walked slowly,
she was very dirty, and there was blood on the side of her

face. But Alan knew who she was.

'Jane,' he said. '*Jane!* Are you all right?'

Jane looked along the platform and saw him. '*Dad?* Why

Alan knew who she was.

are you here?' She walked towards him shakily.

'I came to find you,' Alan said. 'Oh God, Jane, what happened? Did Anna try to kill you?'

Jane touched the blood on her face. 'Yes. She tried to shoot me but she missed. Then I threw her in front of a train. I killed the other one, too.' She smiled, a strange, shaky smile. 'You said there was no justice in this life, didn't you, Dad? Well, those two terrorists murdered five people, and took away your leg and . . . and now they're dead! So there is *some* justice, Dad, isn't there?' Then her eyes filled with tears, and she sat down, suddenly, on a platform seat. 'That woman hated you, Dad,' she whispered shakily, 'really hated you.'

Alan wheeled his chair close to her and held her hands in his. 'I'm so sorry,' he said. 'Anna hated everyone, not just me. But she doesn't matter now, Jane. You're alive! That's all that matters to me. That's all that matters in the world.'

GLOSSARY

artificial not natural; made by people

bastard *(slang)* a bad or cruel person (usually a man)

bloody bleeding or covered in blood; also, a word used to show
that you are angry

boot the place at the back of a car for luggage

chest the top front part of your body

click a short sharp sound

coach a kind of 'car' pulled by horses

confess to say that you have done something wrong

cruel not kind; bringing pain or trouble to other people

damn a word that shows you are angry

doll a children's toy that looks like a person

electric using electricity (power that can make light, heat, etc.)

embarrassed feeling uncomfortable or ashamed about what
other people will think

escalator stairs that can move and carry people up and down

expect to think or believe that something will happen

God (my God!) words you say when you are very surprised

grab to take hold of something quickly and violently

guard *(n)* someone who watches and keeps a building safe

hell (who the hell?) a question showing you are surprised or
angry

hesitate to stop for a moment, showing that you are not sure
about what you are doing or saying

human a person, not an animal

innocent not having done wrong

judo a kind of fighting sport

justice when bad people are punished and good people are saved

kick *(v)* to hit something or someone with the foot

kidnap to take somebody prisoner in order to get money or other things from their family

kiss *(v)* to touch someone lovingly with your lips

look after to take care of

make love to have sex

mews a building (in a town) for horses

ordinary usual; not special or different in any way

parliament the building where a country's laws are made

platform the part of a station where you get on and off trains

port a town or city next to the sea where boats stop

proud feeling pleased about something you have done

queen the most important lady in a country

rope very thick, strong string

shoulder the part of your body between your neck and your arm

sigh *(v)* to breathe out slowly when you are sad, tired, etc.

signal *(n)* a message without words, using sounds, flags, radio, etc.

stare *(v)* to look very hard at something for a long time

stroke *(v)* to move your hand slowly and gently over something

tears water that comes from the eyes when you cry

terrorist someone who uses violence (kidnapping, bombing, etc.) to get what they want

throw (past tense **threw**) to move your arm quickly to send something through the air

tie *(v)* to fasten two things together with rope

transmitter the part of a radio that sends signals

trust *(v)* to believe that someone is good, honest, etc.

tunnel a long hole underground, e.g. for trains

underground below the ground; also, the underground railway

van a kind of big car or small covered lorry for carrying things

Justice

ACTIVITIES

Before Reading

1 Read the back cover, and the story introduction on the first page of the book. They will give you the answers to six of the questions below. Find the questions, and answer them.

1 Where did the bombing happen?
2 What was Alan Cole doing when the bomb went off?
3 Why was Jane Cole in the crowd?
4 Was the Queen hurt?
5 How many people were hurt?
6 How badly was Alan Cole hurt?
7 Who were the five people who died?
8 Which country were the terrorists from?
9 What hasn't Alan realized yet?

You will find the other three answers in Chapter 1.

2 Can you guess how the story ends? Choose one of these ideas. Which ending would be the best justice? Why?

1 The terrorists are caught and sent to prison.
2 The terrorists are shot by the police during a chase.
3 Jane Cole kills the terrorists.
4 Alan Cole kills one of the terrorists.
5 The terrorists kill Jane Cole.
6 Another bomb explodes and kills Alan Cole.
7 Nobody ever catches the terrorists.

While Reading

Read Chapter 1. Answer the other three questions from
Activity 1 in *Before Reading*, and then look at these sentences.
Are they true (T) or false (F)? Change the false sentences into
true ones.

1 At the moment when the bomb exploded, Jane was saying
   something to the American tourists.
2 Jane was badly hurt while helping to save her father.
3 Jane cared more about her father than anyone else in the
   world.
4 The doctors were unable to save Alan's leg.
5 Alan will probably ride, swim, and climb again.
6 Alan heard about his dead friends, and was very angry.

Read Chapter 2, and then answer these questions.

1 Why did the police arrest the two Irishmen?
2 Why was Alan in the Mews the night before the bombing?
3 How long had Alan known Anna?
4 How did Jane feel about her father's new woman friend?
5 Why had Alan written a letter to Anna?
6 Why did Jane decide to take the letter, not post it?
7 What did Jane find out at 14 Bowater Gardens?
8 What did Jane think when she first saw the woman in her
   flat?
9 Why did Jane stop fighting?

ACTIVITIES: *While Reading*

Before you read Chapter 3, can you guess what the man and the woman do next? Choose one of these ideas.

1 They steal the valuables from Jane's flat and then go away.
2 They kidnap Jane and take her out of the country.
3 They keep her prisoner in a house somewhere in London.
4 They kill her.

Read Chapters 3 and 4. Complete these sentences with the right names.

1 _____ soon realized who _____ and _____ were.
2 _____ wanted to kill _____ and get out of the country that night, but _____ wanted to talk to _____ first.
3 When _____ picked up the phone, he heard first _____'s voice, then _____'s voice, and then a scream from _____.
4 _____ realized that _____ had put the bomb in the coach, but he was afraid to say anything because of _____.

Now match these halves of sentences. Who said these words? To whom? When?

1 'If you scream, . . .
2 'If you say a single word about me to the police, . . .
3 'If I don't get away from them soon, . . .
4 'If I speak, . . .
5 . . . you'll find her body in the river Thames.'
6 . . . they'll kill her.'
7 . . . I'll put a bullet through your head.'
8 . . . I'm going to die.'

Before you read Chapter 5, can you answer this question?

The chapter title is '*You must believe me!*' Who do you think will say this, to whom?

Read Chapter 5. Match each question-word to a question, and then answer the questions.

How / What / Where / Who / Why

1 . . . didn't the police think that Anna was a terrorist?
2 . . . did the police find Jane's handbag and flat keys?
3 . . . did Jane free herself from the bed?
4 . . . did Jane do with Kev's cup of hot coffee?
5 . . . killed Kev with his own gun?

Before you read Chapter 6, can you guess what happens next? Choose Y (yes) or N (no) for each of these ideas.

1 Anna comes running upstairs with a gun. Y/N
2 Jane leaves the house and goes to the hospital. Y/N
3 Jane meets Anna in an underground station. Y/N
4 Anna goes to the hospital and tries to shoot Alan. Y/N

Read Chapter 6, and complete these sentences in your own words.

1 The police discovered where Anna was when _____.
2 Halfway down the escalator, Jane _____.
3 Jane hid in a hole in the tunnel wall, but _____.
4 When the train came towards Jane, she _____.
5 All that mattered to Alan was that _____.

After Reading

1 Use the clues to complete this crossword with words from the story.

1 To touch lovingly with your lips.

2 Terrorists kill people with these.

3 A kind of fighting sport.

4 To believe someone is honest.

5 Alan wrote this, to Anna.

6 A telephone does this.

7 Very unkind.

8 Jane lived in one of these.

9 To hit with your foot.

10 To murder.

11 Jane was tied up with this.

12 An animal that pulls a coach.

13 The opposite of love.

14 To take hold of violently.

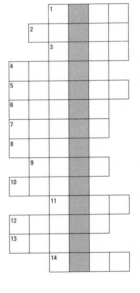

Now you should find a sentence of four words, reading down the dark boxes.

1 What is the sentence?

2 Who said this to Jane, and where?

3 What did Jane think that the person was doing at the time?

4 What was the person really doing?

5 What happened next?

2 **Look at these sentences. Which advice would Jane choose, do you think? Which would *you* choose? Why?**

  1 If you are kidnapped, you should . . .
    a) pretend to be ill.   b) try to escape.   c) wait for help.
  2 If the kidnappers speak to you, you should . . .
    a) not answer.   b) answer politely.   c) shout at them.
  3 If the kidnappers tell you to do something, you should . . .
    a) do it at once.   b) refuse to do it.   c) argue about it.
  4 If the kidnappers get angry with you, you should . . .
    a) stare at them.   b) look at the floor.   c) start to cry.

3 **What did Anna and Kev say to each other when they met after the bombing? Put their conversation in the right order, and write in the speakers' names. Begin with number 6.**

  1 _____ 'In hospital. The radio said that he's lost a leg. But he'll start to wonder about you soon, won't he?'
  2 _____ 'Yes, a student flat in north London.'
  3 _____ "Forget the transmitter. We've got a new problem. Cole isn't dead! The other three are, but not Cole.'
  4 _____ 'No, he won't, Kev. He's in love with me.'
  5 _____ 'Good! We kidnap her, and tell Cole to keep his mouth shut. Do you know where she lives?'
  6 _____ 'Your stupid transmitter, Kev! It didn't work!'
  7 _____ 'In love? Don't be stupid, Anna! The man's lost a leg. He'll put two and two together, and he'll talk.'
  8 _____ 'Oh no! Why did it have to be him? Where is he?'
  9 _____ 'Right, let's get moving, Anna!'
  10 _____ 'So how do we stop him? Ah! His daughter Jane!'

4 Here are some extracts from police telephone calls or radio messages. Choose one suitable word for each gap, and then put the extracts in the right order for the story.

1 'Cole's changed his story. He now says that his girl friend is one of the _____ and that she's _____ his daughter. Send some men to _____ the woman's house and the daughter's _____. Got a pen? Here are the addresses . . .'

2 'We're in South Kensington _____. Just seen a woman with red-brown _____ going down the _____. She's in a great hurry. We're going after her . . .'

3 'Detective Hall has just been to see Cole again. Cole has repeated that he was _____ in the Mews that night. And he isn't seeing this woman any more.'

4 'We've just heard that a _____ has exploded outside _____ and has destroyed the Queen's _____. Get every man down there at once!'

5 'Inspector Lee? We're in Jane Cole's flat now, and we've just found her _____ with her flat _____ in it. It's a bit _____ for her to go out without them, isn't it, sir?'

6 'The _____ at the Mews thinks that Cole had his new _____ friend with him that night, but he isn't sure. Cole has said _____ about this woman. Let's talk to him again.'

7 'I'm at the hospital now. Alan Cole is the only _____ who is still _____, but I can't speak to him yet. His leg was very badly _____ and the doctors have had to cut it _____.'

5 **Perhaps Jane sent a quick email to her brother in Australia to tell him about the kidnap. Complete her email for her (use as many words as you like).**

A lot has happened since you phoned, Philip. When I went back to my flat, the two terrorists who _____. The woman was _____, who had put _____. They said that they _____ if Dad said _____. In the end I escaped, and both the terrorists _____. The man was killed by _____ and the woman was hit by _____. Must get back to Dad now. I'll tell you more later. Love, Jane.

6 **Do you agree (A) or disagree (D) with these ideas? Why?**

1 Jane was as much of a murderer as Anna and Kev.
2 It is always wrong to use violence to get what you want.
3 A 'terrorist' for one person can be a 'freedom fighter' for another person.

7 **Are some of these crimes more serious than others? Put them in order, 1 to 6, with number 1 for the most serious crime. How would you punish each person? Explain why.**

• A terrorist whose bomb kills five people and hurts forty.
• A bank robber who shoots dead an armed policeman.
• A drunk driver who kills a child in a road accident.
• A wife who buys a gun and kills her violent husband.
• A gunman who goes crazy and shoots ten people in a shop.
• A crazy gunman who shoots ten children in a school.

ABOUT THE AUTHOR

Tim Vicary is an experienced teacher and writer, and has written several stories for the Oxford Bookworms Library. Many of these are in the Thriller & Adventure series, such as *Skyjack!* (at Stage 3), or in the True Stories series, such as *The Brontë Story* (also at Stage 3), which is about the lives of the famous novelists, Charlotte, Emily, and Anne Brontë.

Tim Vicary has two children, and keeps dogs, cats, and horses. He lives and works in York, in the north of England, and has also published two long novels, *The Blood upon the Rose* and *Cat and Mouse*.

OXFORD BOOKWORMS LIBRARY

Classics • Crime & Mystery • Factfiles • Fantasy & Horror
Human Interest • Playscripts • Thriller & Adventure
True Stories • World Stories

The OXFORD BOOKWORMS LIBRARY provides enjoyable reading in English, with a wide range of classic and modern fiction, non-fiction, and plays. It includes original and adapted texts in seven carefully graded language stages, which take learners from beginner to advanced level. An overview is given on the next pages.

All Stage 1 titles are available as audio recordings, as well as over eighty other titles from Starter to Stage 6. All Starters and many titles at Stages 1 to 4 are specially recommended for younger learners. Every Bookworm is illustrated, and Starters and Factfiles have full-colour illustrations.

The OXFORD BOOKWORMS LIBRARY also offers extensive support. Each book contains an introduction to the story, notes about the author, a glossary, and activities. Additional resources include tests and worksheets, and answers for these and for the activities in the books. There is advice on running a class library, using audio recordings, and the many ways of using Oxford Bookworms in reading programmes. Resource materials are available on the website <www.oup.com/bookworms>.

The *Oxford Bookworms Collection* is a series for advanced learners. It consists of volumes of short stories by well-known authors, both classic and modern. Texts are not abridged or adapted in any way, but carefully selected to be accessible to the advanced student.

You can find details and a full list of titles in the *Oxford Bookworms Library Catalogue* and *Oxford English Language Teaching Catalogues*, and on the website <www.oup.com/bookworms>.

THE OXFORD BOOKWORMS LIBRARY
GRADING AND SAMPLE EXTRACTS

STARTER • 250 HEADWORDS

present simple – present continuous – imperative –
can/cannot, must – *going to* (future) – simple gerunds ...

Her phone is ringing – but where is it?

Sally gets out of bed and looks in her bag. No phone. She looks under the bed. No phone. Then she looks behind the door. There is her phone. Sally picks up her phone and answers it. *Sally's Phone*

STAGE 1 • 400 HEADWORDS

... past simple – coordination with *and, but, or* –
subordination with *before, after, when, because, so* ...

I knew him in Persia. He was a famous builder and I worked with him there. For a time I was his friend, but not for long. When he came to Paris, I came after him – I wanted to watch him. He was a very clever, very dangerous man. *The Phantom of the Opera*

STAGE 2 • 700 HEADWORDS

... present perfect – *will* (future) – *(don't) have to, must not, could* –
comparison of adjectives – simple *if* clauses – past continuous –
tag questions – *ask/tell* + infinitive ...

While I was writing these words in my diary, I decided what to do. I must try to escape. I shall try to get down the wall outside. The window is high above the ground, but I have to try. I shall take some of the gold with me – if I escape, perhaps it will be helpful later. *Dracula*

... *should, may* – present perfect continuous – *used to* – past perfect –
causative – relative clauses – indirect statements ...

Of course, it was most important that no one should see
Colin, Mary, or Dickon entering the secret garden. So Colin
gave orders to the gardeners that they must all keep away
from that part of the garden in future. *The Secret Garden*

STAGE 4 • 1400 HEADWORDS

... past perfect continuous – passive (simple forms) –
would conditional clauses – indirect questions –
relatives with *where/when* – gerunds after prepositions/phrases ...

I was glad. Now Hyde could not show his face to the world
again. If he did, every honest man in London would be proud
to report him to the police. *Dr Jekyll and Mr Hyde*

STAGE 5 • 1800 HEADWORDS

... future continuous – future perfect –
passive (modals, continuous forms) –
would have conditional clauses – modals + perfect infinitive ...

If he had spoken Estella's name, I would have hit him. I was so
angry with him, and so depressed about my future, that I could
not eat the breakfast. Instead I went straight to the old house.
Great Expectations

STAGE 6 • 2500 HEADWORDS

... passive (infinitives, gerunds) – advanced modal meanings –
clauses of concession, condition

When I stepped up to the piano, I was confident. It was as if I
knew that the prodigy side of me really did exist. And when I
started to play, I was so caught up in how lovely I looked that
I didn't worry how I would sound. *The Joy Luck Club*

Chemical Secret

TIM VICARY

The job was too good. There had to be a problem – and there was.

John Duncan was an honest man, but he needed money. He had children to look after. He was ready to do anything, and his bosses knew it.

They gave him the job because he couldn't say no; he couldn't afford to be honest. And the job was like a poison inside him. It changed him and blinded him, so that he couldn't see the real poison – until it was too late.

The Last Sherlock Holmes Story

MICHAEL DIBDIN

Retold by Rosalie Kerr

For fifty years after Dr Watson's death, a packet of papers, written by the doctor himself, lay hidden in a locked box. The papers contained an extraordinary report of the case of Jack the Ripper and the horrible murders in the East End of London in 1888. The detective, of course, was the great Sherlock Holmes – but why was the report kept hidden for so long?

This is the story that Sir Arthur Conan Doyle never wrote. It is a strange and frightening tale . . .

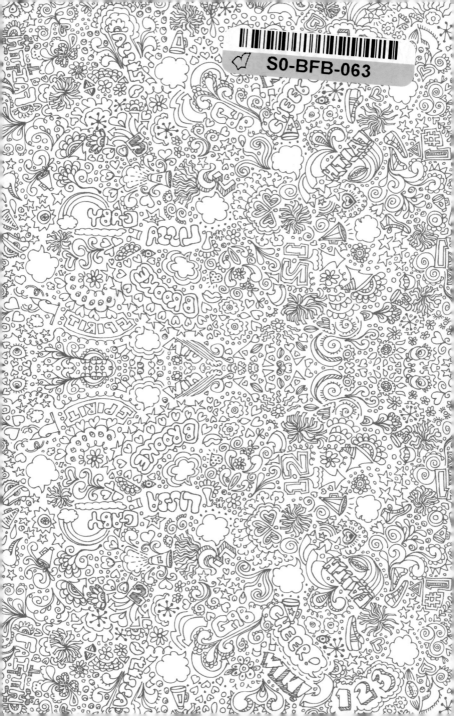

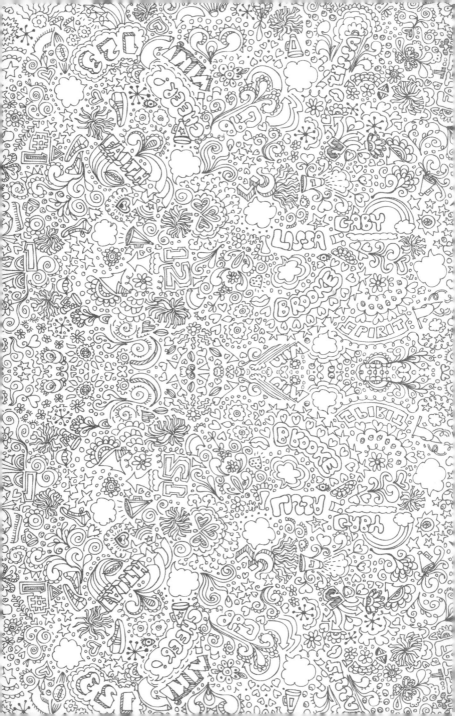

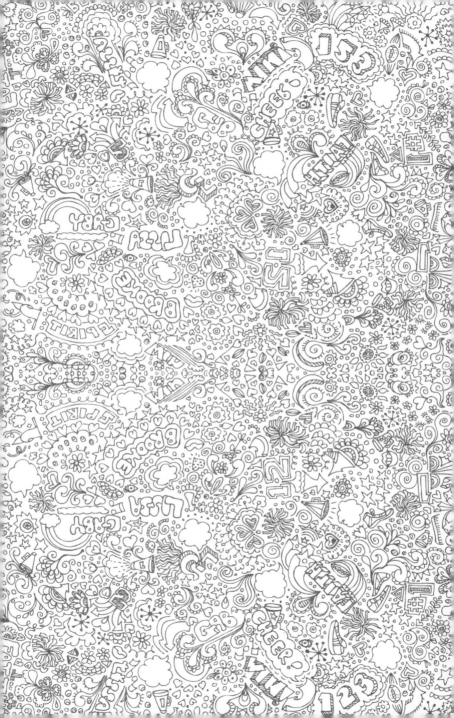

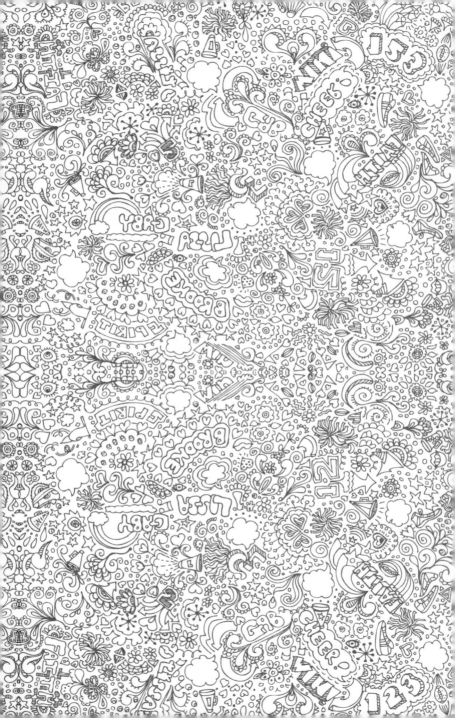

Lissa and the FUND-RAISING FUNK

Team Cheer is published by Stone Arch Books
A Capstone Imprint
1710 Roe Crest Drive
North Mankato, Minnesota 56003
www.capstonepub.com

Library of Congress Cataloging-in-Publication Data
Jones, Jen.
  Lissa and the fund-raising funk / by Jen Jones.
    p. cm. -- (Cheer!)
  Summary: Lissa Marks is the fund-raising chair for her middle school cheer team,
but will her widowed mother be able to afford to keep Lissa on the team?
  ISBN-13: 978-1-4342-4251-8 (paperback)
  1. Cheerleading—Juvenile fiction. 2. Fund raising—Juvenile fiction. 3. Middle
schools—Juvenile fiction. 4. Hispanic American children—Juvenile fiction. 5.
Single-parent families—Juvenile fiction. 6. Friendship—Juvenile fiction. [1.
Cheerleading—Fiction. 2. Moneymaking projects—Fiction. 3. Middle schools—
Fiction. 4. Schools—Fiction. 5. Hispanic Americans—Fiction. 6. Single-parent
families—Fiction. 7. Friendship—Fiction.] I. Title. II. Title: Lissa and the
fundraising funk.
  PZ7.J720311Li 2011
  813.54--dc22   2011001996

Cover Illustrations: Liz Adams
Artistic Elements: Shutterstock: belle,
blue67design, Nebojsa I, notkoo
Cheer Pattern: Sandy D'Antonio

Printed in the United State of America in Stevens Point, Wisconsin.
032012   006678WZF12

Lissa and the

FUND-RAISING FUNK

by Jen Jones

capstone

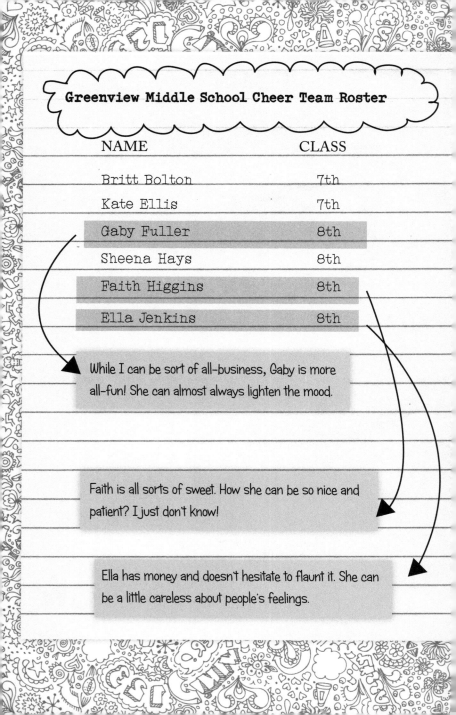

Greenview Middle School Cheer Team Roster

NAME	CLASS
Britt Bolton	7th
Kate Ellis	7th
Gaby Fuller	8th
Sheena Hays	8th
Faith Higgins	8th
Ella Jenkins	8th

While I can be sort of all-business, Gaby is more all-fun! She can almost always lighten the mood.

Faith is all sorts of sweet. How she can be so nice and patient? I just don't know!

Ella has money and doesn't hesitate to flaunt it. She can be a little careless about people's feelings.

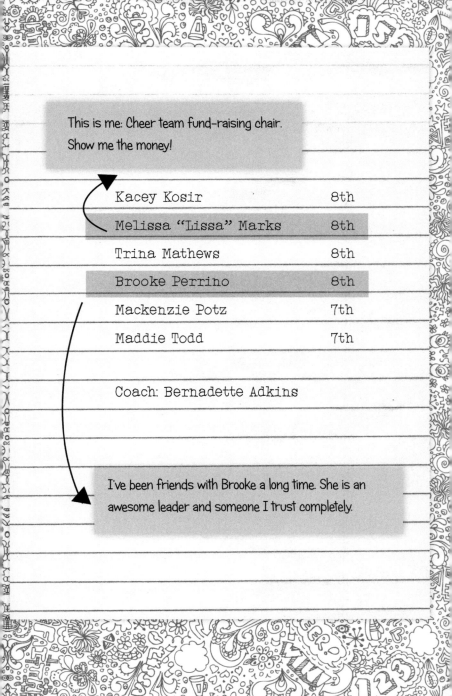

This is me: Cheer team fund-raising chair.
Show me the money!

Kacey Kosir	8th
Melissa "Lissa" Marks	8th
Trina Mathews	8th
Brooke Perrino	8th
Mackenzie Potz	7th
Maddie Todd	7th

Coach: Bernadette Adkins

I've been friends with Brooke a long time. She is an awesome leader and someone I trust completely.

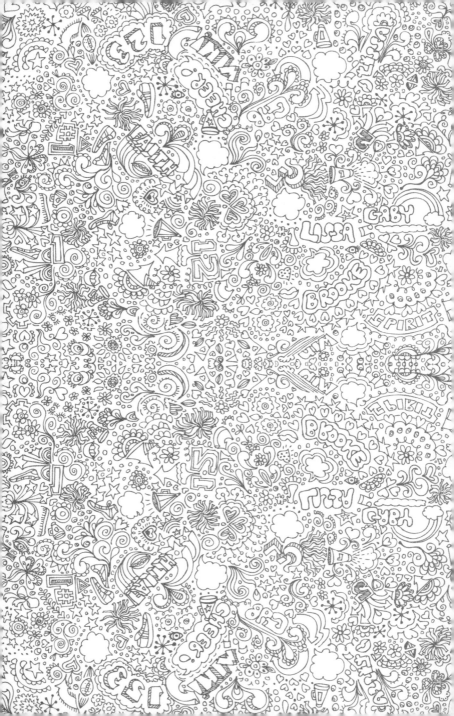

Chapter 1

All dressed up and no place to go? More like surrounded by dresses and wishing I could be anyplace else! There I was, in about the millionth frilly dress store of the day. So far, I'd spent the whole day watching my sister, Dulci, try on gown after gown for her *quinceañera*.

We were throwing a huge party to mark my sister's fifteenth birthday. According to our Hispanic traditions, it was her passing into womanhood. I knew that it was a big deal. But if this was what turning fifteen was all about, I'd rather stay in eighth grade!

"So, what do you think?" asked Dulci, twirling and strutting in some sort of pink lace number. My mom nodded in approval, while I stared longingly out the window at the sporting goods store across the street. It was far more my speed.

Dulci caught my eyes narrowing and followed my gaze. "Last time I looked, Lissa, you were a cheerleader, not a star basketball player," she huffed, rolling her eyes.

The short list of the stores Dulci dragged me to . . .

- Distinctions
- Emily's Designs
- The French Door
- Fun, Flirty & Formal
- High Maintenance
- Irene's Dresses
- Julie Ann's
- The Red Carpet
- Simple Elegance
- Tres Chic Boutique

I scrunched my nose in response. If there was one thing that really got to me, it was when people believed that cheerleaders weren't really athletes. I'd like to see *them* try a tumbling pass or partner stunt! And Dulci was one to talk, anyway. Despite being a cheerleader herself, her idea of exercise was power walking at the mall with her clone friends.

"Yeah, I *am* a cheerleader, and I'm supposed to be at practice in less than two hours, so can we please speed along this never-ending shopping spree?" I shot a pleading look at my mom. I was totally over the dress marathon. Plus, I needed to walk Dixon, my bulldog, before heading off to practice.

"Girls, we're in public! Please try to get along for once," my mom said, hushing us. "Dulci, let's try to narrow this down so we can get Lissa there on time. Which ones are your favorites so far?"

Dulci let out a big sigh and gazed over the gown. "I love them all! I don't know if I can even decide today," she said as she continued to twirl around.

"Come on! Just pick one already," I pleaded. "You cannot torture us with another day of shopping." If I didn't get out of that shop soon, I was going to blow.

Finally, Dulci held up a cream bubble dress and a princessy pink one. My mom took the gowns from her, moving the material around to find the price tags. Her face fell upon seeing the cost.

"These are each more than four hundred dollars," said Mom with a frown. "Doesn't anyone make affordable clothes anymore?"

"Maybe if you shop at a thrift store," said Dulci, flopping onto the dressing room's flowered love seat. "Mom, this is one of the biggest days of my life! I need to look amazing. Plus, most of my friends are spending, like, a thousand dollars on theirs."

I folded my arms. "Way to make Mom feel bad!" I said, giving her an annoyed look.

Dulci should have known better. We were always struggling to make ends meet, ever since my dad passed away six years earlier. Mom was a paralegal at a local law firm, and it was completely on her shoulders to support us.

"No one is looking forward to the quinceañera more than me, *mija**," said Mom. "But these dresses are really pushing it budgetwise."

* mija = my daughter; it's my mom's way of saying "sweetie"

Dulci started whining again, so I rummaged through Mom's purse for her phone. "Be right back," I said, but Mom and Dulci didn't notice. They were too busy debating the dress options. I snuck outside to call my friend Gaby. If only I had my own phone! Lots of my friends had them, but surprise, surprise — my family couldn't afford more than one cell phone.

She answered on the first ring. "***Qué pasa, mamacita**?***" said Gaby. My friends loved to use the Spanish expressions my mom and I had taught them.

"I'm going *loco!* **" I answered, letting out a big sigh. "Turning sixteen may be sweet, but fifteen? Not so much."

Gaby laughed with her cute little giggle. "Dress shopping again?" she asked sympathetically. "Are you sure Dulci's not really my sister?"

She had a point. Gaby was a total girly girl. She loved shopping, makeup, and poring over the latest issues of *Teen*

* Qué pasa, mamacita? = "What's up, pretty lady?" She is too sweet!

** loco = crazy, as in, "Get me out of here now before I go loco!"

Vogue. Me? I'd rather be hiking with Dixon or practicing my **full twist tumbling pass***. Or, of course, hanging with Gaby and our other BFFs, Faith and Brooke. Life was way too short to spend the whole time primping!

"You're more than welcome to take her anytime you like," I said, peeking inside the store to see if they were done yet. "Hey, are we still doing that brainstorming session at practice later?"

Gaby was one of the co-captains of our cheer squad, and I was the fund-raising chair. We hoped that we could all put our heads together to come up with some fund-raising ideas. Competition fees added up fast, and we needed to raise money to cover them.

"Yeah, Coach A said we're going to take fifteen minutes off the tumbling part so we can all meet," said Gaby in response. Coach Adkins was the picture of efficiency. She scheduled our practices down to the minute!

"Cool," I said, as I spotted Mom and Dulci coming out of the shop's doors.

* I'd like my full twist tumbling pass to be my signature move. It's a back flip with the snazzy addition of a 360-degree turn.

Dulci was carrying a plastic bag with the expensive pink dress inside. Somehow she must have talked my mom into it. How did she always manage to get her way? "Hey, I gotta bolt. I'll see you soon!" I said, telling Gaby goodbye.

PRACTICE SCHEDULE

3:15–3:25 ~ Stretching and warm-ups

3:25–3:45 ~ Power jumps and plyometric exercises

3:45–4:15 ~ Stunting / Tumbling

4:15–5:00 ~ Cheer and routine practice

5:00–5:15 ~ Cool down, stretching, and announcements

I stayed quiet the whole ride home. I had to bite my tongue in order not to tell off Dulci. Instead, I just stared out the window at all the BMWs and Range Rovers sharing the road with us. Most of the people in our suburb, Greenview, were pretty well-off. They lived in sprawling new houses. We lived in a modest two-bedroom, closer to the center of the city.

I didn't normally care about that kind of stuff, but some days it was tough to forget about our financial problems. I didn't want my mom to have to stress out about anything. It was hard enough seeing how much she missed my dad all the time. We all did.

When I walked through the front door, Dixon came bounding to greet me. He started running in circles around me, which usually meant he was ready to go outside.

"Honey, you going to let Dixon out?" called my mom, who was still unloading things from the trunk.

"One step ahead of you, Mom," I said, fastening his leash to his collar. "We'll be back!"

As we strolled through the neighborhood, it felt good to take in some fresh air and forget about all things quinceañera for a while. I watched jealously as Dixon sniffed every tree and playfully poked the other dogs we encountered. He didn't have a care in the world. Maybe he could teach me a thing or two.

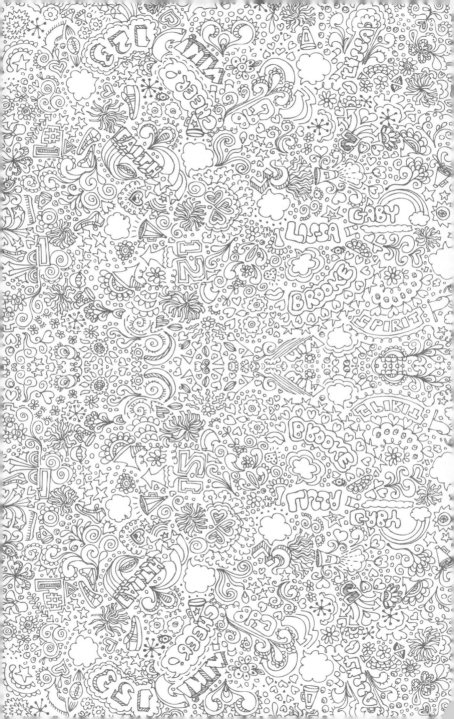

Chapter 2

Despite the shopping marathon and my long stroll with Dixon, I managed to make it to practice on time. And boy, was I glad I did! Coach Adkins was in rare form. "The road to regionals begins here," she barked, adding a little fist pump for emphasis. Sporting military fatigues and a Greenview Vikings baseball cap, she looked every bit the part of drill sergeant.

"Atten-SHUN! I feel some push-ups coming on," said my friend Faith under her breath, getting a little giggle out of Gaby, Brooke, and I, who were all sitting nearby. Faith was usually pretty quiet, so it was fun when she got feisty.

Funny as Faith was, she was probably right. Our practices were no joke — especially when we were preparing for competition. The two hours usually started with a stretching warm-up, followed by power jumps and plyometric exercises. **Plyometrics*** always kicked our butts, but they definitely made our jumps higher!

After that, we usually broke off into separate stunting and tumbling groups. Since I'm a diehard gymnast, you can guess which group I was in! Next was our time to practice whatever cheer or dance routines we were working on. Practices usually concluded with a cool-down, a stretch session, and a quick meeting for any announcements.

As it turned out, today things started a little differently. "Brooke, Gaby, why don't you lead us in our meeting before

* Plyometrics are special exercises that help build all those muscles we use in our jumps. One example is setting up a small cone and jumping over it, back and forth.

we get going?" said Coach A, motioning Brooke and Gaby to the front of the circle.

"Okay, well, we thought it would be inspiring to start off with a round robin of our goals for competition season," said Brooke. "Let's do this thing right! I'll go first. My goal is to be the best leader I can be as your co-captain." She struck a cheesy pose, squinted her eyes, did some spirit fingers, and added a "Superstar!"

"Wow, tough act to follow," joked Gaby. "My goal is to choreograph a rockin' dance routine that the judges won't forget any time soon."

We went around the rest of the circle, and people threw out goals like "Nail my **liberty heel stretch***" and "Lift weights so I can be a more stable base." As my turn came closer, I thought about my own goals. I had lots of them — *perfect my full twist tumbling pass, make up a new sideline chant, learn how to spot stunts* . . . the list went on and on.

---

* One of Brooke's favorite stunts is the liberty heel stretch. As the flyer, she stands with her feet in the hands of two base stunters. They hold her at shoulder level. Then she lifts her right leg high in the air, holding her foot close to her head. She looks amazing!

But my biggest goal? "Making sure we raise enough money to attend the competitions we want," I said, completing the goal circle.

"An excellent transition into our next topic, Marks!" said Coach Adkins. She liked to call us by our last names. "The athletic department budget cuts mean that we'll probably need to do more fund-raising than usual this season. Marks, what has your research turned up?"

I pulled out my bright teal folder of catalog cutouts, magazine articles, and fund-raising ideas from the internet. As the chair, it was my job to present the best options to the team. "Well, after the endless candy drive last year, I'm assuming no one wants to sell chocolate bars door-to-door again."

A collective groan provided my answer. Except for Gaby, of course, who had a notorious sweet tooth. "I wouldn't have minded in the least," she piped up jokingly.

"Okay, so that's a big *ix-nay* on the *ocolate-chay*," I said, making an imaginary 'X' in the air. "Here are some ideas that I thought could be fun. One is to volunteer as grocery baggers at a local store for a day and collect tips for the competition kitty."

Another squad member, Ella, cleared her throat. "Um, I don't do minimum wage-style jobs," she said. She could be really snobby sometimes. "Can't we just set an amount and require each family to pay a competition fee?"

"Yeah, seriously, it would save us a lot of time that could be spent practicing instead," said Kacey. She always echoed whatever Ella said.

Faith gave me an "it's okay" look. She knew that there was no way that my mom could afford that. I felt my cheeks turn red, and my temper starting to flare up.

Luckily, Coach Adkins jumped in before I could shoot back a retort. "Ella, fund-raising isn't just about making money," she said. "It's also about team building and working together toward a common goal." Ella just shrugged. "Who else has suggestions?"

We tossed around some more ideas, like selling bracelets with our school name and hosting a team dinner for fans. But no *one* idea really seemed to click with the whole squad. I was

MY DOs AND DON'Ts OF FUND-RAISING

DO . . .

. . . tell people WHY you are raising money. What will it be used for?

. . . ask local businesses if they are willing to be a sponsor.

. . . wear your uniform or school colors. Show the people who are donating that you support your school.

. . . be friendly and outgoing. People are more likely to help out nice kids who are treating others with respect.

DON'T . . .

. . . go door-to-door without a buddy. Stay safe!

. . . act all giggly and silly. It will look like you aren't serious about reaching your goal, plus adults will be annoyed with you.

. . . don't expect your parents to do all the work. It isn't their job to make you cupcakes for a bake sale or vacuum cars out at a car wash.

. . . forget to say thank you to your donors.

getting a little frustrated, but I was also determined not to let the meeting end without a plan in place.

"Okay, how about this?" I proposed. "What if we do a cheer clinic for some of the elementary schools? We would charge a small fee and teach some basics. I bet they would let us use the gym." I saw a few heads start to nod and smiles start to emerge. Could it be we might actually have a winner?

"Aww, I bet the little kids would be so cute," said Sheena with a big grin. "I know I would have loved something like that back in the day!"

"Yeah, and when they grow up, they can be Greenview cheerleaders!" said Gaby, and everyone laughed. "It's like secret recruiting."

"Not to mention that we'll get to cheer instead of having to sell things to people," said Brooke, always the practical one. "It would be a cool way to try out some new material."

"Case closed, then! A cheer clinic it is," said Coach A, making some notes on her clipboard. "Brooke and Gaby, you'll meet with Lissa to finalize the details soon, yes?"

We all nodded in agreement. With anyone else, it

might feel like work, but planning stuff with your best friends was just pure fun! And with Gaby's upbeat energy, Brooke's strong leadership skills, Faith's unwavering support, and my determination, we all brought something needed to the table.

"We're doing a sleepover at my house this weekend, so we can work on it then," Brooke told Coach Adkins.

"Fantastic!" said the coach, checking her watch. "We're running behind, so stunting and tumbling time it is."

> **Stuff we need to figure out for the Cheer Clinic!**
>
> – Who will we invite?
>
> – Day and time?
>
> – How much should we charge?
>
> – Can we use the school gym?
>
> – How should we get the word out?
>
> – Do we need snacks? Can we find someone to donate them?
>
> – Is there an event where the little girls can perform and show off all they have learned?

I scurried over to my cheer bag to get my wrist supports. No better time to start working on my goal of hitting my double full twist! And now that we had a fund-raiser in place,

I had an extra spring in my step. After all, I didn't know what I would do if I couldn't afford to be part of this squad! So I'd put my whole heart and soul into making this fund-raiser the most successful one yet.

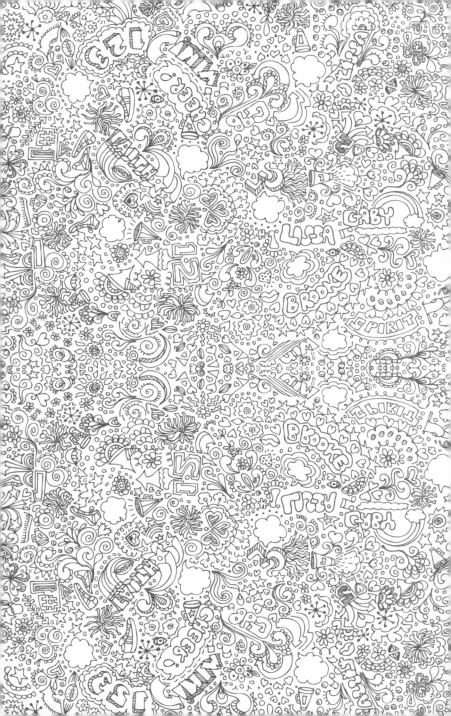

Chapter 3

Friday usually meant one of two things: a pep rally or a sleepover at Brooke's house. And on really great weekends, it meant both! This particular week, our football team had a bye, so they weren't playing — and we weren't cheering.

Luckily, it couldn't have been better timing. The break would give us extra time to practice and put the finishing touches on our fund-raiser idea. And what better place to do that than Brooke's house? It was awesome — her family had a big pool and lots of room in the house to lounge around, watch movies, or even practice our moves.

"Did you remember your swimsuit, Liss?" asked my mom, who was driving me over to Brooke's place. "And I hope you packed your allergy pills. You know how I worry about Brooke's cats." I was deathly allergic to cats. It was weird, because dogs weren't an issue at all for me. I could bury my face in Dixon's fur with no prob!

"Yes, I've got everything, Mom," I said. "I did forget to pack the kitchen sink though." I shot her a sly smile.

"Very funny," she said, smiling in spite of herself. "That's good, because I don't have time to turn around and get anything. I have to make it to the bakery by six o'clock to finalize the cake details."

"Ooooh, are we doing a red velvet tower?" I asked, licking my lips. I was already mentally saving a piece for Gaby, too.

"With all the trimmings," my mom answered. "Even though it's tragically overpriced."

I wasn't surprised. Planning a quinceañera was practically like planning a wedding. Think of all the details in a typical wedding day. A quinceañera had loads of the same special touches. The invitations, the dress, the cake,

Ms. Ines Marks
requests the honor of your presence
at a Mass celebrating the
fifteenth birthday of her daughter
Dulci Ernestina
on Saturday, the tenth of September
at five o'clock in the evening at
Holy Family Church.
Reception immediately following at
Holy Family Reception Hall.

the church, the bouquet . . . even a "court" that was like a bridal party!

My mom mistook my silence. "Don't worry, mija, you'll be having your own quinceañera before you know it," she said as we pulled into Brooke's driveway.

"Oh, I'm in no rush!" I said, laughing. Parading around in a tiara and Cinderella-style ball gown was about as appealing to me as quitting the cheer squad. Although, I couldn't deny there was something kind of cool about the traditional parts of my heritage.

"Thanks for the ride," I added, giving my mom a kiss and grabbing my duffel bag. "See you *mañana**."

"*Hasta luego***," my mom called out the window as I bounded toward the doorstep. I was suddenly feeling full of TGIF energy!

As it turned out, Faith and Gaby had already arrived and were lounging by the pool with Brooke. It was funny . . . each girl's bathing suit totally reflected her personality. Faith was wearing a classy one-piece halter suit, while Brooke was rocking a daring bold print bikini. And of course, Gaby was wearing a cute polka dot two-piece with ruffles, her hair in pigtails. Luckily, I'd worn my own Adidas racing suit under my clothes and was ready to take the plunge!

"Hey! We were just about to text you to see when you were getting here," Brooke said.

———————

* mañana = tomorrow

** hasta luego = see you later

"Yeah, we were almost ready to put out a 'Missing Cheerleader' memo," said Gaby, making a reach for Brooke's sunscreen.

"Sorry, my mom doesn't get out of work until 4:30 on Fridays," I explained. "You know, that whole bringing-home-the-bacon thing and all."

"Mmmm, bacon," said Gaby. "What's for dinner, anyway?" She raised an eyebrow at Brooke.

"My mom mentioned something about a spinach lasagna," said Brooke. Her family was Italian, and they usually did pasta night on Fridays. When Brooke hosted a sleepover, we always looked forward to dinner.

"Well, we want to be able to really enjoy our food later, so we should get down to business?" said Gaby. She was normally goofy, so it was extra cute when she tried to be all businesslike.

"Only if I can give my expert feedback from the pool!" I answered, tearing off my tank top and sweats. "I'm dying to take a dip." I was kind of the sporty one of the group. I'd much rather do laps than sit in the sun doing nothing.

"Deal," said Brooke. "I'll join you." She took a little running start and did a cannonball into the water.

"And I'll take notes," offered Faith. "Since I'm the only non-officer here, I might as well make myself useful."

Over the next hour or so, we managed to nail down the details for the cheer clinic. The formula was simple: the two competitions we wanted to attend cost about $35 per cheerleader, so the clinic had to raise about $850.

Add in matching hair bows, accessories, makeup, and other extras for the twelve of us, and the fund-raising goal was closer to $1,000. And that was just

$35 x 12 = $420 per competition

$420 x 2 = $840

for the first few competitions! After that, we'd need to raise money for regionals, and then maybe even for nationals if we did well.

"Okay, so here's how it breaks down," read Faith from her notes. "On Monday, Brooke and Gaby will finalize the clinic date with the athletic director and make sure the gym is good to go. Once that's all set, I'll design flyers, and we'll assign people to hang them around town and in school. We'll also organize a committee to contact the elementary schools in the area and invite their students."

"And don't forget that someone needs to make up a cheer, chant, and dance to teach the kids. I can definitely help with that!" said Gaby. She was our choreography queen. "Hey Liss, maybe we could get Dulci and a few of the high school cheerleaders to teach some material?"

"Uh, maybe," I said. Dulci and I did practice and do moves at home sometimes, but lately we'd had *way* too much togetherness. This was *my* baby! "We'll also need some parent volunteers to work the door and collect forms, waivers, and checks," I added, looking for a way to change the subject.

"Count me in," said Brooke's mom, coming up behind us with a tray of fruity drinks. "Lissa, your mom's on the phone, sweetie." She handed me the cordless, and I walked inside so I could hear better.

"Mom, what's up? Everything okay?" I asked.

"Oh, mija, you missed all the drama," said my mom. "I was coming back from the bakery when the car completely broke down in the middle of traffic. It was smoking and everything! Luckily, I'd grabbed the cell phone from Dulci earlier so I was able to call a tow truck."

"Oh, no!" I exclaimed. "Is everything okay now?"

"Well, I'm fine, but the car will be in the shop for a while," said my mom. "The reason I'm calling is to see if you can get a ride home tomorrow from one of the girls."

"I'm sure we can work something out," I said her. I was glad I could relieve her of at least one small worry.

"Tell them *gracias** for me," said my mom. "You girls having a good time over there?"

"It's more of a working sleepover," I told her. "We're ironing out the details for the fund-raiser."

"Good thing," said my mom. "This car problem is probably going to cost a couple thousand dollars. We'll need all the help we can get."

I felt an ache in the pit in my stomach. If Dulci's quinceañera didn't drain all of our meager funds, this unexpected car issue probably would. I hastily said goodbye to my mom and

---

*gracias = thank you, but you probably already know that from your days with Dora

went to join the girls on the patio. They were sharing the scoop on the fund-raiser with Brooke's mom.

"Lissa, I'm very impressed with this plan you've put together," said Mrs. Perrino, seeing the sour look on my face. "Sounds like you girls really have it all figured out."

I could only hope so. Since I was the fund-raising chair, the outcome definitely reflected on me, but most people had no idea why holding the title really meant so much to me. More than ever, I was counting on these fund-raisers to be successful. Otherwise, I'd be stuck sitting on the sidelines. And that was about the least cheerful thing I could imagine.

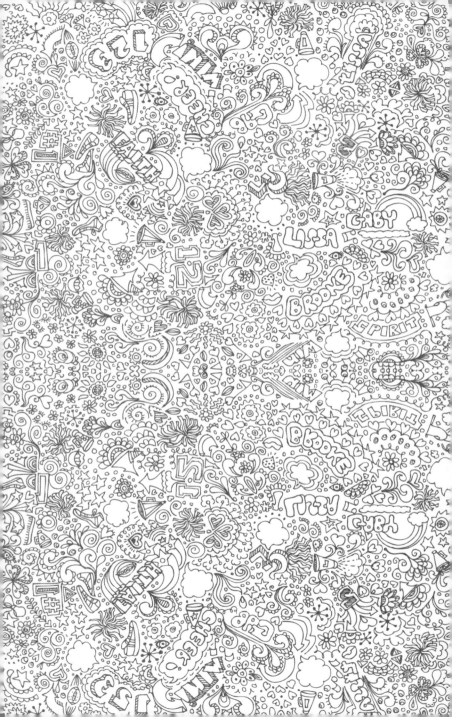

Chapter 4

I'm not gonna lie. The starter stretch at cheer practice can sometimes be a little boring. (After all, you want to get to the good stuff!) But after an all-nighter, a nice stretch is often just what the cheer doctor ordered. "Sooooooo sleepy," Faith grumbled as Trina and Mackenzie led the group in a series of leg stretches.

We'd had a blast at Brooke's the night before, watching old chick flicks and dancing around like dorks. Gaby was even convinced that during the night we were visited by "Johnny's ghost," an inside joke among the four of us.

Johnny Campbell was a legend in the cheerleading world. He'd started the first cheer squad ever at the University of Minnesota back in the late 1800s. According to Gaby, Johnny's ghost seemed to make an appearance at every one of our sleepovers!

So what cheer did good old Johnny excite the crowd with back in November of 1898?

RAH, RAH, RAH!
SKI-U-MAH!
HOO-RAH! VARSITY!
MINN-E-SO-TAH!

That's just classic!

I didn't *totally* rule out the possibility. But I was sure that if Johnny did have a ghost, it would have better things to do than to haunt the Greenview Middle School cheer team.

"I'm telling you, Johnny was walking around in the attic all night," said Gaby, leaning over to touch her right toe.

"Girls," said Coach Adkins, hovering over us, "unless you want to write an essay about the history of cheerleading, I suggest you stop talking about Johnny Campbell and stretch yourselves out properly."

She knew us too well. And she did have a point. Today

we not only needed to assign tasks for the fund-raiser, but we also needed to start learning our competition routine.

The routine turned out to be super cool. Coach Adkins had hired a local choreographer to put it together for us, and Gaby was going to add in the dance routine portion. Today the choreographer, Trent, was here to teach us the opener. If *he* was any indication, it was sure to be dazzling. He was a cheerleader at the local community college, and *whew*, was he cute!

The first step was to learn the starting formation. Usually we started with the two stunt groups in back doing some sort of pyramid or partner stunts, while the four gymnasts crossed the front with eye-catching tumbling passes. Trent had some other ideas about how to shake things up.

"Okay, so, Lissa, Kate, Maddie, and Britt, you're going to start at the back of the mat," said Trent, motioning us to go to our positions. "Stunt partners, you're going to hit four **single-base toss chairs***, while the tumblers pass through the

---

* Let's break down the single-base toss chair. You have one base and one flyer. The base tosses the flyer up, catching her with one hand above the head. The flyer bends one leg and keeps the other straight, with the base pushing up on that straight leg for extra lift. Still not sure? Look it up on YouTube.

windows." He went on to match up the flyers — Brooke, Gaby, Ella, and Trina, with their bases, Mackenzie, Sheena, Kacey, and Faith.

It sounded pretty cool. Basically, we would be traveling through the open spaces between each stunt and end up in front of the formation. I raised my hand. "What's the **tumbling sequence***?"

"**Round-off, back handspring, layout****," answered Trent without missing a beat. Once we all understood the idea, we practiced several times just "marking" the moves, or basically faking it to get the feel of the formation and timing. Then it was time to try it for real!

Coach Adkins hit play on the iPod dock. Trent had put together an upbeat '80s mix of high-energy songs

---

* A tumbling sequence features two or more gymnastics skills, like a round-off followed by a back handspring and finished with a layout.

** This sequence starts with a round-off, a cartwheel that ends with the legs snapping together and feet landing at the same time. From there, the tumbler goes right into the back handspring, springing back onto her hands, then over onto her feet again. Then to get the layout in, she heads into a back flip.

like "Mickey" and "Material Girl." (Of course, these were speeded-up versions that sounded like they were on caffeine.)

At the beginning, we yelled "HEY, VIKINGS!" over the singer's "Hey, Mickey." It was a really cute approach, and we were going to wear floppy gold hair bows to drive the theme home.

"Five, six, seven, eight!" yelled Brooke, after which we all hit **toe touch jumps*** for the first move of the routine. The tumblers hit regular jumps in the back, while the bases lifted the flyers so that their jumps would look mega high. Together, it was a cool visual effect. Following the jumps, the stunts loaded in while we took a running start for the tumbling pass.

It was always tricky to synchronize tumbling, but somehow we made it work. The round-off happened during the

* If jumping isn't your strong suit, a toe touch can be a bit intimidating, but with some practice, you'll be soaring soon. Also, plyometric training really helps you develop height so you can get those legs straight out and to the side, arms reaching to touch the toes.

1-2, the back handspring on the 3-4, and the layout on the 5-6. We used the last two counts to spin around facing front. At this point, we tumblers would dance while the stunters combined to form two groups of four in back. They'd be doing one of the flashiest stunts of all: **a basket toss***!

It was a lot to learn in one day, but we managed to master pretty much the whole sequence by the end of practice. Having Trent spot me on my layout wasn't too shabby, either! (Just sayin'.) And it was a boost I sorely needed. Between the sleepover and the hard practice, I was ready to take a long *siesta***.

I wasn't just physically exhausted, but emotionally, too. No doubt the week ahead would be a long one. Between helping Mom and Dulci prepare for quinceañera, setting up

～～～～～

* The thing getting tossed in a basket toss is the flyer. Two or three bases throws the girl up, and once she's airborne she hits a trick before falling back into the bases' arms. The crowd is always jazzed to see a basket toss!

** siesta = nap, as in, "I better get a siesta soon, or I am done functioning."

the cheer clinic, and cheering, I was going to be super busy. Time to keep my eyes on the prize ... which would hopefully be a shiny first-place trophy! As soon as we could pony up the pennies, anyway.

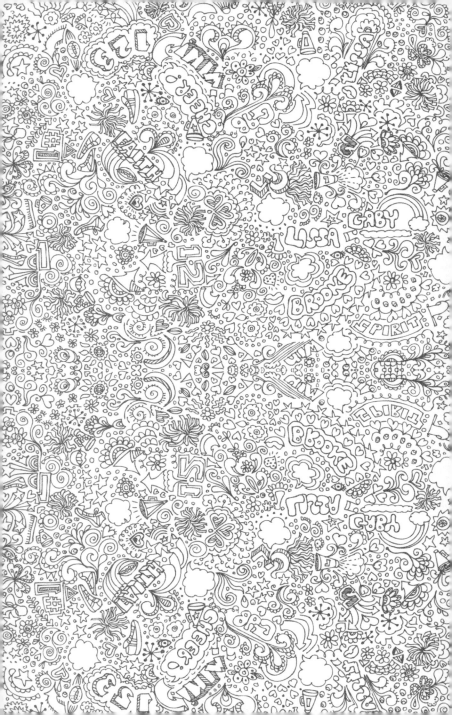

Chapter 5

Study hall was usually a great time to get a head start on homework, but on Monday, I couldn't concentrate. Brooke and I had special permission to leave the computer lab halfway through the period to go hang flyers for the cheer clinic in the halls. Until then, I was counting the minutes! (You can only reread the same page in your history book so many times.)

A tiny window popped up on my computer screen. Finally, something to distract and entertain me for a while. As if reading my mind, Brooke had sent me an instant message:

BPBELLA: I just had a brill idea! Lightbulb, much?

SPICEGRRL: Don't keep me in suspense! I'm over here trying to read up on the reconstruction after the Civil War, but all I can think about is the clinic. Oh, and Trent.

BPBELLA: Trent is *muy caliente** indeed. So here's the idea: what if we have stations at the clinic? We could split the girls up into four groups: jumps, chant/cheer, dance, and gymnastics, then they could rotate around the room.

It really was a great idea. We could even make colorful banners to show which stations were which. It would also help us give the girls more personal attention — more bang for their buck!

SPICEGRRL: Clearly your thinking cap is a designer one! Stellar idea, Perrino.

* muy = very; caliente = hot; put them together and she's basically saying Trent is adorable!

BPBELLA: LOL! You're starting to sound like Coach A, with the whole last name thang.

Before I could shudder at the thought, the study hall supervisor tapped me on the shoulder. "Lissa, you and Brooke are dismissed to go do what you need to do," she whispered.

Woo-hoo! Free at last. I gathered up my backpack and notebooks and went out into the hallway to wait for Brooke. I dug the pack of flyers out to see what Faith had created. Printed on bright neon yellow paper, they looked great! The info was short, sweet, and to the point — perfect! Faith had also included spirited star graphics, scattered all over the page.

I made a mental note to designate Faith our squad's unofficial graphic designer. She was awesome at that sort of thing.

"Looks good," said Brooke as she exited the study hall room and snuck a peek. "You've got the flyers, I've got the sticky tape. We should be all set!"

LEARN TO CHEER!

Don't know a Herkie from a hurdler?
Is high V just another letter in the alphabet to you?

Come learn the basics of cheerleading
from championship squad Greenview Middle School!

WHAT: Cheer Clinic taught by Greenview Middle
Cheer Team

WHO: 3rd through 6th graders welcome

WHEN: October 7th, 11 a.m. – 2 p.m.

WHERE: GMS Gym

HOW MUCH: $15/person

WHY: Cause cheerleading rocks! Plus, your
generous donations help the team raise
money for competition.

All participants are invited to perform with us during
halftime at the Greenview/Forest Park football game
that evening.

GO VIKINGS!

We spent the next half hour hanging flyers in the hallways, cafeteria, gym, and on school bulletin boards. Of course, we also needed to save some to hang up in all of the elementary schools. "Liss, you free to go to Dunbar and Revere with me and Gabs after school?" asked Brooke, reading my thoughts again.

"No can do," I told Brooke with a frown. "Duty calls. My mom needs my help preparing the party favors for Dulci's big day."

"What are you making?" asked Brooke curiously.

"Dulci wants mini-tealight decorations for everyone to keep, so we have to place the candles inside the holders and put them in frilly bags," I told her. "It seems like whatever Dulci wants lately, she gets. And don't even get me *started* on her tiara. Um, Miss Universe called, and she wants her blingin' crown back."

Brooke laughed. "Do I get to be in your quinceañera court when it's your turn?"

"No doubt. You'll be the queen!" I said, waving an imaginary wand in the air like I was Brooke's fairy godmother.

"But of course, darling," said Brooke, curtseying. The bell rang, signifying it was time to get to our next classes. "And just like that, the bubble bursts."

As other students started to fill the halls, Brooke taped one last flyer to a locker and turned to me. "Can you ask your mom if she'll be one of the parent volunteers for the clinic? We've got Trina's, Kate's, and my mom on board, and we still need one more."

"Count on it!" I said, heading toward my science classroom.

The rest of the day flew by, and I hurried home so I could walk Dixon and help out as promised. Except I arrived to an empty house. My mom and Dulci were nowhere to be found. Even Dixon seemed less excited than usual to see me. He'd been snoozing on his doggie bed before I got home.

I kept myself busy for the next hour by writing in my journal and listening to some chill music. It was kind of nice to have the bedroom all to myself without Dulci around. But I was a little annoyed. I could have gone to hang flyers with the girls if I'd known they were going to be late. Where were they?

Dulci's laugh trailed in from the driveway. *Finally!* I thought. *Grrrr.*

My mom walked in the door, holding fresh flowers. She seemed to be in a great mood, unlike me. "Hi Lisa-belle," she said, calling me by her special nickname for me. "Sorry we're late. We got held up at the florist."

I tried not to show my frustration. "What did you get?" I asked.

"We picked out corsages

My favorite artists to just chill to . . .

* Adele
* The Avett Brothers
* The Bird and the Bee
* Bruno Mars
* Death Cab for Cutie
* The Fray
* Florence and the Machine
* Glee (the slower songs)
* Jack Johnson
* Jason Mraz
* Mumford & Sons
* Postal Service
* She & Him
* Vampire Weekend

and boutonnieres for the court, plus lots of flowers to decorate the church," said Dulci, burying her nose in Mom's bouquet.

Even her simplest actions annoyed me. "Everything's coming together really nicely!" she added.

I bet, I thought. They certainly seemed to be spending all their time on the quinceañera these days!

"How was your day, Lissa?" asked my mom.

I began to tell her, but Dulci interrupted. "I'm going to go upstairs and get all the crafting materials for the party favors," she said.

"You do that," I said, irritated. It was always the Dulci show when she was around!

"As I *started* to say, it was pretty good. Everyone's getting really excited for the cheer clinic," I said.

"That's great, honey!" said my mom. "I'm sure you'll raise lots of money for the team. What day is it again?"

"Saturday, October seventh," I answered. "Oh yeah, that reminds me, would you be able to be one of the parent chaperones?"

"I wouldn't miss it," said my mom, bending down to kiss the top of my head. "Can I learn the cheers too?"

"Why not? I'm sure you'll be a natural. After all, I had to

get all my awesome moves from *somewhere*," I joked. "We'll pencil you in for the seventh."

"Put it in ink," said my mom. "I can't wait!" And neither could I.

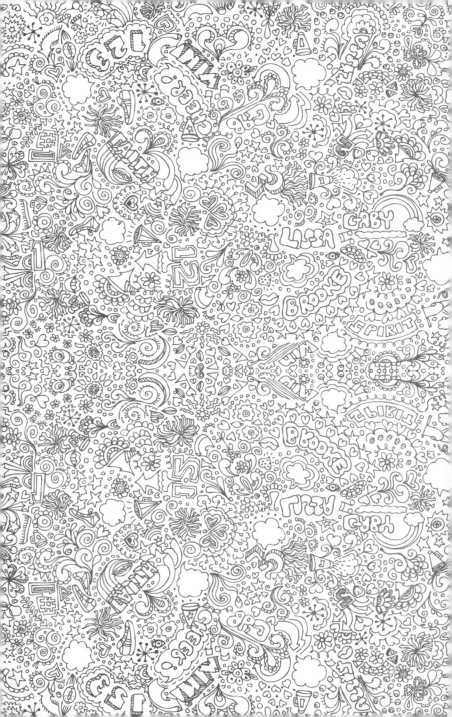

Chapter 6

The day had finally come, and I was crossing my fingers that all would go well with the cheer clinic. (If toes could be crossed, I would have crossed them, too!) The response so far had been pretty impressive, with 32 girls signing up ahead of time. That put us almost halfway toward our fund-raising goal. I could only hope that we'd have plenty of walk-ins!

Mom and I had to take a cab to school, so by the time we got there, the gym was already buzzing. Sheena, Faith, and Kacey were hanging up banners, while Brooke and Gaby were deep in conversation with Coach Adkins. Mackenzie was testing the microphone and speakers, while Kate and Britt were unfolding the gymnastics mats. It was definitely a team effort.

"What do you think they need me to do?" asked my mom. She looked pretty tired. I realized she'd probably been burning the candle at both ends between working all the time and catering to my and Dulci's needs. I felt grateful that she'd given up one of her weekend days to help us.

"Let's walk over to the check-in table and see if you can set up shop there," I said, guiding her toward the gym entrance. Brooke's and Kate's

The BIG DAY!

Don't forget to . . .

- Get there at 8:00. We still have a few things to set up.

- Wear practice uniform with shorts.

- Get banners hung; Coach A is bringing them.

- Test the sound system.

- Greet the parents . . . and thank them!

- Have hand-outs ready for the girls: review sheets and directions about the evening's performance.

- Bring my list of who's doing what. I need to know what's going on!

moms were already there, putting out the safety waivers and sign-in sheets.

"Hi, Ines!" Mrs. Perrino greeted my mom. "You're just in time. Can you count the money we'll be using to give change?"

"Sure," said my mom, taking a seat at the table by the collection box.

"Thanks for helping out," I said to all the moms. "As the fund-raising chair, I can officially say on behalf of the whole team that we definitely couldn't do it without you!" I felt a little cheesy, but it was true. Without the support of fans and cheer parents, most squads wouldn't make it very far.

"Lissa!" Coach Adkins called from the other side of the gym. "We need you over here, please."

"You're in demand," said my mom, with a smile. "Don't worry about us. We've got everything under control."

"Yes, ma'am," I said, doing a little salute and heading over to see Coach A. She didn't waste any time getting to the point.

"Marks, you're the captain of this ship, so we need you to make sure things sail smoothly from the start," she commanded. "I want you to do a welcome speech for the girls and get the energy flowing. Can you handle that?"

"You know it," I said, offering a salute in response. Coach A nodded authoritatively and went off to bark at someone else. She cracked me up sometimes.

Gaby came running up breathlessly in her place. "Okay, I think all the I's are dotted and the T's are crossed," she said. She was really embracing the whole captain thing.

"Well, sounds like you've got it all covered from A to Z," I teased her.

"Very funny, Liss," she said, making a funny face at me and cocking her head. "Want to go over the cheer and fight song one more time before the participants get here?"

"Sounds like a plan," I told her. Gaby and I had worked together to make up a new cheer and create an easier version of our fight song choreography. Since we only had a half hour at each station, we had to make everything pretty simple so there would be enough time to teach and review the material.

"Yo! Greenview girls!" I yelled in my loudest cheer voice. All by itself, it seemed to echo off the walls of the gym.

"Whatever you're doing, take a break because we need to go over the routine." Even though not all of us were teaching at the cheer and dance stations, it was important that we all know the material well in case the participants had any questions. Plus, we'd all be performing it together at the game that night!

Everyone quickly got into formation. **"READY?"** called Brooke. **"SET!"** the rest of us yelled.

VIKES, LET'S HEAR YOU YELL
WE WANT A WIN
WE WANT A WIN!

VIKES, LET'S HEAR YOU SPELL
G-M-S
G-M-S!
G-M-S, LET'S WIN IT!

Scattered applause came from around the gym where our parents and the other volunteers were watching. Coach Adkins cued up the fight song music, and we continued our practice performance. Some of the girls messed up a little. They were used to our normal choreography for the fight song. Unfortunately, we hadn't had tons of time to practice our clinic material, since we'd been so busy getting our competition routine ready. But after going over it a few times, everyone felt pretty solid. And thankfully so . . . people were starting to arrive!

As girls began to trickle into the gym, we put on some upbeat music over the loudspeakers. It was important to get the energy high before we got going! Gaby came up next to me and put her arm around my shoulders. "We did good, kid!" she said.

I couldn't help but agree as I surveyed the crowd. There were a few elementary school cheer squads, plus individual girls who just wanted to learn more about cheerleading.

Some of the girls started clapping to the music and forming cheer circles. Most of our Greenview squad joined in, but I held back. I was too busy trying to count the number of girls in the gym. But I stopped myself before I got too far. I didn't want to worry about how much money we were making before we even got started. It was time to put the "fun" in "fund-raising!"

Coach Adkins walked up and handed me the wireless microphone. "It's show time," she said, granting me a rare smile.

As she turned down the music, the cheers died down and the crowd looked toward me. Suddenly, I was super nervous. How could that be? I performed in front of dozens — even hundreds — of fans all the time and felt totally at home in the spotlight. Speaking on my own was proving to be an entirely different story!

NERVES!
How to handle 'em.

- Take a few deep breaths to calm yourself down.

- Practice. If you know what you're doing, you won't be as scared.

- Remember that your audience wants you to do well. They are having a good time watching you and will appreciate your performance or speech.

I cleared my throat. "Welcome to our Greenview Middle School cheer clinic!" I greeted everyone. "I'm Lissa Marks, and I'm the squad fund-raising chair. By being here today, you're helping make our competition goals happen. So thanks for your support!" Everyone clapped politely, and I felt better.

"Now who's ready to cheer?" I shouted, trying to sound more confident. The loud whoops and yells that answered me lifted my spirits. "I *said*, who's here to cheer today? If you're ready, get up on your feet!"

The crowd erupted in loud cheers again, and my teammates started doing high kicks, jumps, and flips to rev up the girls. Coach A was right. It really was show time!

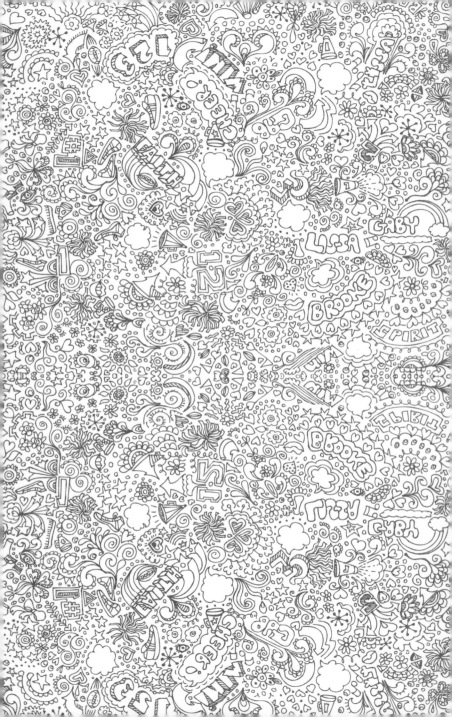

Chapter 7

Phweet! Coach Adkins's whistle blew, meaning that it was time to change stations again. We'd already made it through two rounds, and the girls seemed to be having a blast. I was assigned to the gymnastics area, but I kind of wanted to visit the other stations and see how things were shaping up.

"Maddie and Britt, can you guys hold down the fort for a few minutes? I want to go check on the others," I said. At their nods, I followed the group of girls leaving our station over to the jumps station, where Faith, Ella, and Trina were running the demo.

"Hey, F, what's up?" I asked Faith. She was stuck teaching alongside the two biggest divas on our team, so I wanted to make sure she was hanging in there okay. She and Ella didn't have the greatest history.

"I'm loving this!" she said, her face beaming. "The girls are so cute."

I couldn't help but

JUMPS WE WILL TEACH

toe touch

Herkie

pike

*Note: If the group of girls is less experienced, consider teaching:

spread eagle

pencil jump

tuck

agree. I'd totally fallen in love with one of them, a fourth grader named Adeline, while helping her learn a cartwheel. Sharing our own love of cheer was *so* much fun, I couldn't believe we were actually getting paid to do it!

"I know. And they are all sweeties, too," I said. "This makes me want to be a cheer camp instructor when I'm old enough."

Ella's voice cut in. "Sweet lovefest and all, but we should probably get started," she said, giving us the eye. She wasn't exactly the picture of warm fuzzies.

"Don't let me stop you," I said, holding my hands up in an exaggerated way. She didn't intimidate *me*. "You've got the floor!"

Ella stepped forward. "Greetings, munchkins!" she addressed the younger girls. We'd divided things up so that two of the stations had third and fourth graders, and the other two were filled with fifth and sixth graders. Still, "munchkins" was a bit much! Of course, it was kind of a *Wizard of Oz** reference, and she wasn't really that far off from the Wicked Witch, so maybe it did fit. Ha!

"We're going to show you three different kinds of jumps,"

---

* I have always loved the munchkins in The Wizard of Oz, but the flying monkeys? Not so much. (They are totally freaky, right?!) So when we watched the movie when we were little, Dulci used to sit on me, trying to force me to watch every second of the big monkey scene. Another reason older sisters stink!

Ella continued. "First, a Russian, or **toe touch**." Faith did a flawless toe touch to show what one looked like. She always managed to get amazing height! "Next, a **Herkie**," prompted Ella, as Trina demonstrated the classic jump. "And finally, one of the *hardest* jumps, the **pike***," said Ella, as she prepped for a pike jump. Her legs and arms met in the air in front of her, toes perfectly pointed.

TIPS FOR TACKLING JUMPS!
(pass along to the girls at the clinic)

- Be sure to stretch . . . and stretch often!

- Practice plyometrics. These are exercises that build your leg muscles so you jump higher.

- Make sure you are properly warmed up before tackling jumps.

- When you are just learning a jump, have a friend give you a boost. She can place her hands on your waist and help lift you so you get extra height.

---

* Where do your hands and feet end up for each jump? Toe touch: Legs out to sides, parallel to the ground, while hands reach out toward toes. Herkie: One leg is straight and slightly to the side. The other leg is bent with the knee facing down. The arms vary. Pike: The body is bent with the arms and legs reaching straight out in front.

"As cocky as she can be, she does have the goods to back it up," I whispered to Faith, who nodded reluctantly.

"Do you guys want to learn how to do these jumps?" Trina asked the girls watching, all of whom responded with enthusiastic answers of "Yeah!"

LUNCH MENU

Sandwiches
(turkey, ham, or veggie)

Fruit platter

Veggie tray

Pasta salad

Frozen yogurt for dessert!

Time was ticking away, so I decided to go visit the other stations. Following this round, we would break for lunch, and after that, we'd only have one more station to go. Then we'd finish the clinic with a large group practice and the girls performing for each other. It would be good prep for the half-time show that night!

But before I could reach the cheer station, Coach Adkins intercepted me. "Marks, let's talk," she said, pulling me aside. "I've got the final numbers, and I thought you might be interested in hearing them."

I felt my chest tighten. By my count, it seemed that there

were plenty of girls there, but would it be enough to cover all of our competition costs?

"The total head count is 46 participants," said Coach Adkins. "Minus our overhead costs, that brings us to a total of $625, which I think is pretty darn good. Don't you?"

Doing the mental math, I realized we were still $375 short of the original fund-raising goal. "Definitely," I answered, trying to hide my disappointment.

"You should be proud of yourself, Lissa," said Coach Adkins, apparently sensing my mood shift. "It's not easy to put on and promote an event like this. This is a true success!"

"I'm thrilled, really," I insisted, feeling my face flush. "I'll be right back. I'm going to run to the restroom real quick!"

I hurried toward the hallway, trying not to be upset. She was right. It really had gone off without a hitch so far, and everyone deserved a pat on the back. But I couldn't shake this horrible, nagging fear that our families would be stuck paying the remainder. Sure it would only be around $30 for these first few competitions, but the season was long from over. There would be more fees to come, and that was a major problem — at least for me.

I shut myself into a bathroom stall, letting a few tears slide down my cheeks. I felt like a baby, but I was tired of worrying about money all the time. And I had to admit, it didn't seem fair that Dulci's quinceañera fund seemed to endlessly flow, while we pinched pennies everywhere else. I knew the tradition was really important to my mom and our relatives, but still! Cheerleading was really important to me.

"Liss?" I heard footsteps and Brooke's voice carry over the stalls. "Coach A sent me to see if you're okay."

I tried to dry my eyes quickly, but Brooke was on to me. "Girl, I can hear you sniffling! Come out here and talk to me."

I slowly exited the stall. I felt silly. One, I never cried — at least not in public. And two, deep down inside, I felt like no one else truly understood.

"Hey, B," I finally said, my head hanging down.

"What on Earth are you upset about?" she said, handing

me a tissue. "You're our fearless fund-raising leader, and this is the best event we've had in a long time!"

"I know," I said sheepishly. "I just don't want our families to have to pay a competition fee. This event isn't going to cover it all."

"We'll work it out," said Brooke, trying to make me feel better. "Maybe we can find a local business to sponsor us. There are lots of ways to raise money, so buck up, little camper! You're not alone in this. It's not all on your shoulders." I knew she was probably right. But it sure didn't feel that way.

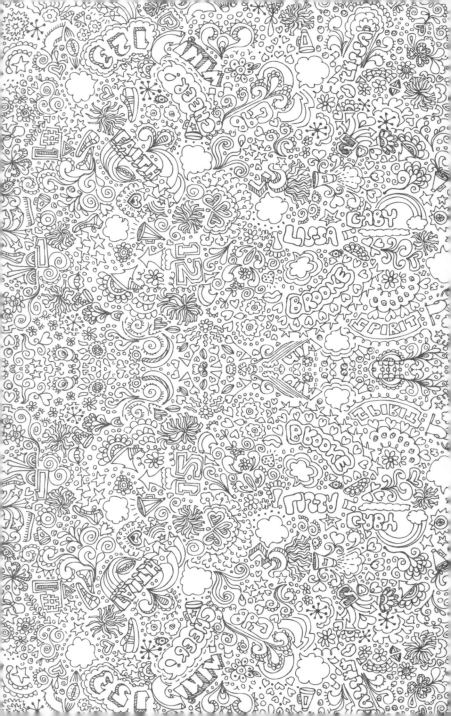

Chapter 8

After the clinic, I hopped a ride with Gaby and her mom. My mom had left after the sign-in part because she had to pick up the car from the shop and take Dulci on some errands. (No shocker there.) When I returned home, Mom seemed eager to see how it all went. "Mija, you did it!" she exclaimed in greeting. "Do we have a whole new generation of cheerleaders on our hands?"

"Looks like it," I said lamely. I didn't really feel like chatting it up. Plus, I couldn't help but notice all the shopping bags on the table, which made me feel even grumpier.

"I'm going to try to take a nap before the game; I'm totally wiped out." And before she could really answer, I started heading up the stairs.

As I snuggled into bed with Dixon curled up at my feet, I prayed that Dulci wouldn't come into our room. A little peace and quiet was definitely in order. But just as I started to drift off, a knock interrupted my slumber. "Hey, Lis-a-belle," said my mom, coming to sit on the edge of my bed. She wasn't going to give up so easily. "Why so sleepy?"

"All that jumping and cheering can wear a gal out," I said, sitting up a little. "You saw us. It was nonstop action from the minute the girls got there."

"I know, I was so proud of you," said my mom. "Especially when you gave your speech. So how much did your team raise in the end?"

I felt myself get all prickly again. I *really* didn't want to talk about this, especially not with my mom. The last thing I needed was to hear her say it wasn't enough.

"We didn't hit our goal, but we'll get there somehow," I said, trying to convince myself more than her.

"I certainly hope so," said my mom. "These budget cuts are completely ridiculous. Now on top of paying for cheer camp, clothes, and everything else, they want us to pay for competitions, too? Why can't cheerleaders get the same privileges as the other sports teams?"

"*Some* cheerleaders get plenty of privileges," I said, glaring toward Dulci's side of the room. I couldn't help it.

My mom raised her eyebrows. "Lissa, I don't appreciate your tone," she said firmly.

"I'm just sick of Dulci's party eating up all our money!" I cried. I knew I was being a baby, but it really didn't seem fair.

"Honey, this is something I've been saving for since you were little girls," said my mom.

"Saving for?"

"Yes. I have special accounts for both of you, so we can pay for your quinceañeras. This is more than just a party. A girl's quinceañera only happens once, and it's something she'll always remember. This isn't only about Dulci — it's about our family, our culture, and honoring it properly.

When you turn fifteen, you'll have your own party, and it will be just as spectacular. Let Dulci have *her* moment."

"But, Mom, we barely get by as it is," I said. "I just worry about everything. And if I wasn't able to cheer . . ." My voice trailed off.

"Try not to fret about it, mija," said my mom. "All sports can be costly. But your happiness and health are a great return on our investment! You know I'll do whatever I can to make sure you can keep cheering. And I appreciate how hard you're working to defray the costs."

It was nice to hear, but I couldn't help but wonder if she was just trying to say the right thing. My eyelids started to get heavy again. "*Te vas a dormir*," said my mom, speaking Spanish for "go to sleep." "Get some rest before the game." And just like that, I drifted off into dreamland.

A few hours later, the alarm jolted me out of my siesta. And speaking of time, was the clock right? Because, if so, I was ultralate! I glanced over at Dulci, who was sitting on her bed reading an issue of *Seventeen*. "Aggghh! I totally over-slept," I complained, burying my face in the pillow.

"Oh, I pushed the snooze button for you a few times," said Dulci. "You were totally out, so I figured I'd let you rest a bit."

"Are you loco?" I asked. "The game starts in less than an hour, and the squad has probably already started practicing! Plus, we have to lead all the girls from the clinic in the half-time show."

"Sorry," she said, shrugging. "I was only trying to help."

I just shook my head. I didn't have time to argue! Grabbing my cheer uniform out of my closet, I ran downstairs. "Mom," I called. "We have to go — now!"

Mom was lying on the couch, the TV on. "What?" she said, rubbing her eyes a little. "Oh, I dozed off myself."

I held up my uniform. "I'm really late for the game. Can you take me to the field? I'll just change there. Coach A is going to be so mad at me!"

"Oh, no!" she said, sensing my urgency. "Do you have your shoes and your cheer **briefs***?"

* We wore briefs to make sure our underpants and bottoms were well covered. One time Gaby was especially spacey and forgot to put hers on before a game. Well, someone reminded her after the first stunt, and needless to say, she has not forgotten since!

"Ugh! My cheer bag is still upstairs," I said, groaning. "I'll be back in a flash!"

"Meet me at the car," instructed Mom, who was already putting on her shoes. "I'll have Dulci walk Dixon."

I left my uniform on the couch and flew up the steps. If ever there was a need for speed, the moment was now!

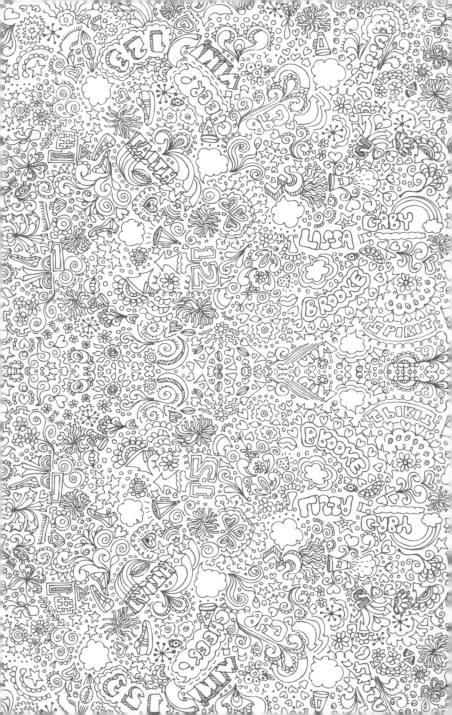

Chapter 9

The car barely came to a stop before I flung the door open.

"Thanks, Mom!" I called, giving her the quickest kiss ever.

"No problem," she called after me as I ran toward the field. I could see the team practicing in the parking lot, and Coach Adkins's cap gleaming in the distance. Let's hope I didn't get in too much trouble!

I sprinted up behind Coach Adkins. "Coach, I . . ." I started, out of breath.

"About time, Marks!" Coach said, but she was smiling. What had gotten into her today, anyway?

I opened my mouth to explain again, but Coach quickly shooed me into position. They were about to practice the routine again from the top. As I got into formation, something felt off. Staring around, I noticed that a few of the team members were missing. What the heck? Maybe I wasn't the only **Rip Van Winkle*** of the bunch. I tried to shoot Brooke a quizzical look, but she had already started the cheer.

"**READY?**" she called.

"**SET!**" we yelled back as we launched into the familiar motions. After teaching the same cheer all day, it was old hat by now! We ran through the fight song too, just marking it since we didn't have the music to play. It would be really fun to perform this with all the girls from the cheer clinic. We'd be like one giant team.

After a few more run-throughs, Coach Adkins told us to take a break. Soon it would be time to regroup on the field

* Do you remember the story of Rip Van Winkle? He goes into the mountains to avoid his nagging wife, but ends up falling asleep for like 100 years. Lately, I think missing 100 years would totally be worth it to avoid Dulci.

for game start. After a bathroom detour and quick change into my uniform, I bolted up to Brooke. "B!" I said. "Where are Faith, Gaby, and Mackenzie?"

"Oh, yeah, let's go look for them," she answered, a mischievous smile on her face. "I'm sure they're around here somewhere." Something was definitely up. First Coach Adkins was bordering on nice, and then Brooke didn't seem concerned that a quarter of the team was missing. Time to put on my best Nancy Drew face and figure this one out!

We walked past the concession stand, and I snuck a peek to see if Gaby was there, eating Red Vines. No dice. "So are you feeling better about everything?" asked Brooke. "Where were you, anyway?"

"I totally snoozed the day away by accident," I admitted.

> Gaby's favorite place at a school game:
> The concession stand!
>
> She loves:
>
> • Red Vines
>
> • M&Ms
>
> • Lollipops
>
> • Snickers
>
> • Starbursts
>
> • Anything that has sugar as one of its first three ingredients.

"The clinic and being all upset really took it out of me. I do feel a little better now, though."

We kept walking, and we'd barely made it past the ticket stand when I spotted the MIA cheerleaders. They were standing behind a table, and Gaby was painting something on a fan's face. As we got closer, I noticed a sign on the table that read:

VIKING FACE FLAIR
JUST $2!

I felt thoroughly confused. All fund-raisers had to go through me, and we certainly never did two in one day! "Hey, how much for some flair?" I said, sneaking up behind Gaby.

She jumped, and her paintbrush accidentally drew a green line across the fan's forehead! Her cute graphic of a Viking helmet was now just a blob. Whoops.

"Lissers!" she said, laughing. She quickly stifled the laugh upon seeing the look on the fan's face. "Oh, sorry about that," she said, reaching for a Handi-Wipe to refresh her canvas.

"What are you guys up to?" I asked. "When did you decide to do face painting?"

"Brooke told us how upset you were that the cheer clinic didn't raise our full competition fees," said Faith. "We talked to Coach A and asked her if we could double up our efforts and try to make some extra cash at the game. This was the easiest way to do it!"

"Yeah, and we've already made close to $120!" said Mackenzie, fanning herself with some dollar bills. "All the girls from the cheer clinic wanted them, and pretty much the whole cheering section, too."

I was overwhelmed with gratitude. Brooke, Faith, and Gaby knew the real reason I was upset. And they wanted to make sure I didn't worry about having to drop out of cheer-leading. So here they were, trying to raise more money. And it really was a perfect idea. This game was even more packed than usual, since all the families from the clinic had come to watch their girls perform. "I can't believe you guys did this," I said, getting a little choked up.

"Hey, turn those tears into cheers," said Brooke, pointing at her cheeks and pulling them upward to make a big clown grin. "You've already cried way more than anyone should in one day." She motioned to the countdown clock on the field. "Plus, we've only got five more minutes! We need to tear this puppy down soon and go make our team tunnel."

It was a tradition we did at the beginning of every home game. We always stood in two straight lines facing each other outside the locker room entrance. At the end of the line, two cheerleaders held up a big run-through sign. Pumped-up music played over the loudspeakers, and the team would then bust through the "tunnel" and sign as they stormed the field. The crowd always went crazy!

Today was no different. As the first notes of "**Welcome to the Jungle***" filled the air, a roar rose from the stands in anticipation. As the football players ran onto the field, we did jumps and tumbling tricks of excitement. I could hear some of the girls from the clinic yelling stuff like, "Go Trina!" "Get it, G-M-S girls!" It was cool to have our *own* fans for once.

In the space of an hour, I'd gone from totally bummed to totally stoked. I still couldn't believe the generosity of my friends, and that they'd gone to the trouble of staging another mini fund-raiser. (And a great idea at that! I made a mental note for the future.)

My biggest fear had always been that I might have to quit the squad if it got too expensive, but I realized now that the odds of that were pretty low. Seeing the way our squad banded together today showed me that we could make it through any challenge, financial or otherwise. And that made my pasted-on cheer smile grow ten sizes more.

---

* "Welcome to the Jungle" is one of those songs that will forever be played during sporting events. It's by Guns & Roses, who my mom is STILL completely obsessed with. Her obsession a little weird.

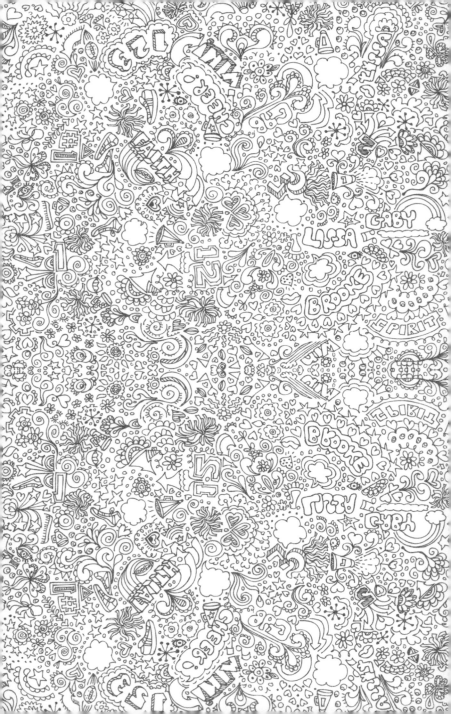

Chapter 10

The game proved to be an exciting one, with both teams scoring lots of points. For every touchdown, we did six pushups, so we'd already gotten plenty of exercise besides our sideline chants! "We shouldn't have to do any conditioning this week," joked Brooke after we hit the ground yet again.

"Try telling that to Coach A." I said, laughing. "Somehow I don't think she'll have any sympathy."

"Hey! Look, Trent came to watch us," said Brooke, pointing toward the stands. Okay, it was official: this game was the *best* one yet! That was so cool of him to come support us. We were going to debut the opening sequence of our competition routine after the cheer clinic performance, so he probably wanted to see the crowd's reaction.

The score at halftime was Panthers 21, Vikings 20, so the energy was crackling when the buzzer sounded. Gaby and Brooke immediately sprang into action. We needed to get performance-ready!

"Britt and Sheena, can you guys go check the stands and make sure we're not missing any of the clinic girls?" asked Brooke. "They're all supposed to meet us at the south entrance to the field, but there could be a few stragglers."

"Copy that," said Sheena, linking arms with Britt.

"Trina, you go make sure the marching band knows the cue," instructed Gaby.

The rest of us walked over toward the south entrance, where lots of the cheer clinic girls were already waiting for us. They looked so jazzed — and so cute with all of their Viking face paintings. Some of them had probably never performed in front of a crowd before. It was going to be fun to be part of that new experience and relive the excitement all over again through their eyes.

Britt and Sheena hurried up with a few extra girls in tow. I spotted Adeline playing with her ponytail and went over to say hi. "Hey, Addie!" I said, giving her a hug. "I had fun tumbling with you today."

"Me too, Miss Lissa!" she said. She was so formal — it was cute. "Watch this." She turned a cartwheel, finishing off the move with a little jump and some spirit fingers. "I've been practicing all afternoon!"

"You *rock*," I told her, giving her a high five. "We'll have to hit the mat again sometime soon."

Suddenly Coach Adkins's voice boomed over the speakers. "Ladies and gentlemen, may I have your attention, please? Today we'd like to welcome some special guests, third through sixth graders from all over the city who attended our cheer clinic. They'll be performing a special halftime show for you now. So without further ado, presenting the Greenview Middle School cheerleaders and their guests, the Viking Spirit Squad!"

I grabbed Addie's hand and we ran onto the field. All the cheerleaders started doing what we call "wildin' out." It's basically just the name we picked to describe our way of getting the fans pumped up. We run around and yell, jump, kick, flip, and basically spaz out! I'm sure that with all the cheer clinic participants behind us, we looked like a major spirit army. We'd even recruited one of the girls' younger sisters, a tiny first grader, to wear a Viking mascot outfit and join us on the field. It was quite a spectacle!

When we reached the center of the field, every-one lined up in formation. We'd decided to just form a bunch of straight lines to make things easier for everyone. Instead of Brooke calling the cheer, we'd given the honor to one of the cheer clinic girls by picking her name out of a hat.

"VIKINGS, READY?" called Christy, a sixth-grader from Dunbar Elementary School.

"SET!" all of us answered. We hit the first motion of the cheer and launched into it:

VIKES, LET'S HEAR YOU YELL

WE WANT A WIN

WE WANT A WIN!

VIKES, LET'S HEAR YOU SPELL

G-M-S

G-M-S!

G-M-S, LET'S WIN IT!

One of the coolest things about the cheer was the crowd participation part. Three of the cheer clinic girls stood at the front of the formation holding signs to prompt the fans. On one side, the signs showed the words "We Want a Win," and on the other "G-M-S." The girls flipped them and held them up during the proper parts of the cheer. They were really getting the full cheer experience!

We finished the cheer with the front lines kneeling and hitting a low V with their arms, the middle lines hitting a T motion and lunging, and the back hitting a high V. The level changes made a striking visual effect. The crowd started cheering us on, and I took the break to catch my breath. As I stared at the crowd, I spotted my mom . . . and Dulci?! She never came to my games! Wow, this day was just getting better and better. I sent a big smile their way, hoping my mom would forgive me for being such a brat before.

After the applause died down, Trina gave the sign to the marching band and they began to play the fight song. We performed the easier version we'd taught that day at the clinic. To add some spice, I did my full twist tumbling pass across the front during the last part of the routine. I was definitely flying high — in more ways than one!

The game turned out to be a loss for the Vikes, but it was hard to put a damper on our spirits. After weeks of preparation, we'd finally pulled off the clinic. To celebrate, Gaby, Faith, Brooke, and I went to grab a smoothie afterward. A little strawberry-banana action was in order!

"So Lissa, how on Earth are we going to top today?" said Faith. "Personally, I think this fund-raiser was way better than peddling chocolate bars door-to-door."

"Mmm, chocolate," said Gaby, taking an exaggerated sip of her cookies-and-cream milkshake. We all giggled. For some reason, that joke never got old.

"To quote Scarlett O'Hara, 'I'll think about that tomorrow,'" I said in a fake Southern accent. "Right now, I'm just enjoying the moment."

And it was true. Fund-raisers could raise hundreds — maybe even thousands of dollars — but these times with my friends? Priceless!

Tell me the truth . . .

I rarely doubt myself. I think it's really important to believe in yourself and your actions. But after this whole fund-raising thing, I realized I might not ALWAYS be right. What do you think?

- Did I have any right to be mad about the amount of money that was going toward Dulci's quinceañera?

- I worked really hard on our cheer clinic. Was there anything you would have done differently to make it a bigger success?

- If you had my money concerns, would you have talked to Coach A about it? Do you think I should have confided in her or my mom even?

I like to check out the forum pages of my favorite cheer magazines to get fund-raising ideas. Sometimes I respond to the questions posted there. Help me write answers to these questions.

My parents hate cheerleading!
posted by cheerwannabe 1 day ago

I told my parents I was planning to go out for cheerleading and they said I couldn't. They think cheerleading is just about meeting boys and showing off in short skirts. How can I convince them it's a great team sport?

HELP! I choke up . . .
posted by nervouspoms 4 days ago

My squad has decided to go around to businesses and ask for donations. I get SO nervous talking to strangers. I'm afraid that I'll just stand there looking confused. Does anyone have any tips that might help me?

Which cheerleader are you?

Quiz: Are you Brooke, Faith, Gaby, or Lissa? Take this fun quiz to find out which cheerleader you're most like.

1. You forget your homework. You:

A. Make sure to talk to the teacher about it privately. You don't want to draw attention to yourself in class.

B. Turn it in the next day, and ask for an opportunity for extra credit so you can make up missed points.

C. Head to the library to tackle it . . . again. Looks like you have to redo it in order to get it in on time.

D. Don't realize it until it's time to hand it in, so you make a joke, give a grin, and promise the teacher you'll turn it in tomorrow.

2. The school play is coming up. You:

A. Volunteer to be a stagehand. You like being involved, but you aren't going to get up in front of anyone.

B. Have no plans to try out. You like to stick to physical extracurriculars.

C. Would love to try out, but will it fit into your busy schedule?

D. Plan to try out. After all, you love to meet new people!

3. You have a free afternoon. You:

A. Paint in your room. You like to spend time by yourself to rejuvenate.

B. Head out for a hike. It will be good exercise.

C. Start with some study time, go on a bike ride, and then finalize plans for the party you're hosting.

D. Work on some new choreography. There are some new dance steps you have been dying to add to the school song routine.

4. Cheerleading tryouts are next week. How do you feel?

A. Uncertain. Cheerleading sounds fun, but the limelight is a little too hot for you.

B. You can't wait. You're going to nail that new tumbling pass.

C. Awesome! After tryouts, you'll be one step closer to becoming captain.

D. Pretty excited . . . you'll be back with your girls, and making new friends, too.

Quiz continues on the next page!

5. Your favorite thing about cheerleading is:

A. Learning a new skill. You had no idea you had it in you.

B. Working toward a common goal, like new uniforms or fees.

C. Helping others learn the cheers and dances so they can do
   their best.

D. Making posters and goody bags for the teams. It's fun to chat
   and hang out as we're working.

6. What role do you fill on the squad?

A. New girl — I'm still figuring it out.

B. Treasurer — I can tell you how much money we have (or need).

C. Leader — I like to make sure everyone is in the know.

D. Social butterfly — I see to it that cheerleading is fun
   for everyone!

7. My family . . .

A. Has a lot of fun coming up with crazy things to do together.

B. Is small, but tight. I can count on my mom for anything.

C. Is proud of me. They encourage me to work hard and be my best.

D. Is loud and fun! It's bound to be, with all those siblings around.

8. When I am with my friends, you can be sure I:

A. Will be a good listener. And if the moment arises, I'll get a laugh or two.

B. Will tell people exactly what's on my mind. I'm sassy like that.

C. Have organized an activity for us. I like making sure everyone is having fun!

D. Will be happy and carefree. And if someone has a fashion crisis, I'll be solving it.

. . . .

If you chose:

----> **Mostly A** — You are Faith. You may be shy, but when you're with your friends or family, you shine with your sweetness and fun sense of humor.

----> **Mostly B** — You are Lissa. You work hard to meet your goals. Best of all, your friends know they can count on you to be honest and supportive.

----> **Mostly C** — You are Brooke. You like to be in charge, and you're good at it. If a friend or teammate comes to you, she knows that you will be happy to help her.

----> **Mostly D** — You are Gaby. You make friends easily and can be counted on to ease the mood. Friends appreciate your spunky style and sheer silliness.

WINNING FUND-RAISERS

If your team's cash supply is nothing to cheer for, don't worry about it. Fund-raisers are a great way to help fill your squad's piggy bank.

Kiddie Clinic

Get ready to teach a group of cheerleaders-in-training! Invite local children to a one-day cheer lesson. They'll love learning simple cheers and dance numbers. Stage a routine for parents at the end of the day.

Amazing Auction

Try to get local businesses to give away freebies for the auction, like vacations, dinners, or trips to the beauty shop. During a sporting or school event, use the lobby to host a "silent" auction, where fans write their bid amounts on paper. It's a win-win situation. Fans go home with great gifts and your squad's piggy bank grows.

Dance-A-Thon

Put on your dancing shoes! Join forces with a deejay or band to stage an all-day dance marathon. Supporters can pledge money for every hour that you boogie down.

* Excerpt from *Cheer Essentials: Uniforms and Equipment* by Jen Jones, published by Capstone Press, 2006

Meet the Author:
Jen Jones

Author Jen Jones brings a true love of cheerleading to her Team Cheer series. Here's what she has to say about the series, cheerleading, and reading.

Q. What is your own cheer experience?

A. I absolutely love cheerleading! I cheered from fifth grade until senior year of high school, and went on to cheer for a semi-pro football team in Chicago for several years. I've also coached numerous teams, and I write for a few cheerleading magazines.

Q. Did any of your family members cheer?

A. Some families are into football — mine is into cheerleading! My mom was a coach for close to 20 years, and my sister cheered throughout grade school and high school. My aunt and cousins were also cheerleaders.

Q. Which cheerleader from the series are you most like?

A. I would say I am probably a combination of Gaby and Brooke: Gaby for her outgoing, bubbly nature, and Brooke for her overachieving, go-getter side. In certain situations, I wish I could channel some of Lissa's feisty fabulousness!

Q. What sort of goals did you have when writing the series?

A. My goals were to create relatable characters that girls couldn't help but like, and also give readers a realistic look at what life on a young competitive cheer squad is like. I want readers to finish the book wanting to be a member of the Greenview Girls!

Q. What kind of reader were you as a kid?

A. I loved to read and often brought home dozens of books every time I went to the library. Whether at the dinner table or in bed, my nose was ALWAYS in a book. Some of my favorite authors were Judy Blume, Lois Duncan, Lois Lowry, Paula Danziger, and Christopher Pike.

Read all of the Team Cheer books

#1-Faith and the Camp Snob

#2-Brooke's Quest for Captain

#4-The Competition for Gaby

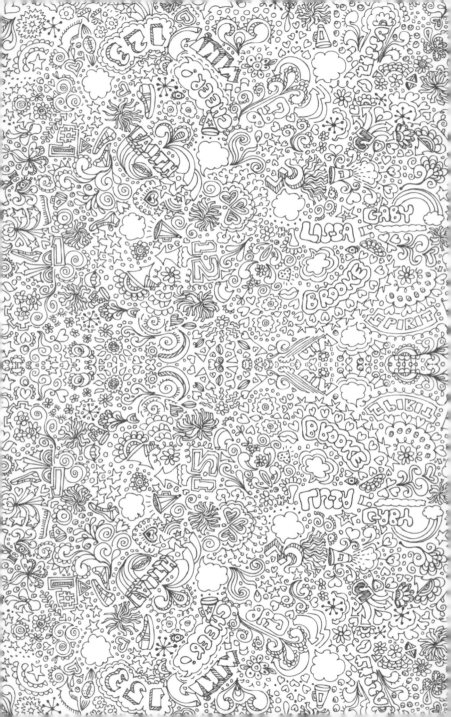

Check out the first chapter from the next book,

The Competition for Gaby!

Being the only girl in a family full of guys might usually turn someone into a total tomboy. But not me. Nope, I was probably one of the girliest girls around!

In fact, my bestie Lissa was way more into boy stuff than I was. That's probably why whenever she came over my house, she ended up throwing footballs with the guys while I soaked up sun. Not that I didn't love hanging around with my four brothers, too. I'd just rather fish for finds at the mall than actually *go* fishing. Know what I mean? That was one of the reasons I couldn't get enough of my dance classes.

It was mostly girls at my studio, so I got to escape Planet Testosterone for a while. Plus, it allowed me to indulge my passion for fashion — whether it's '80s-inspired neon getups or a lime green tutu paired with striped tights. Thankfully our dance studio didn't have a dress code! Back when I was a little kid, I was always stuck wearing a boring bun, black leotard, and pink tights. (Can you tell I had been dancing forever?)

I was at the *barré* stretching when a girl I didn't recognize started warming up next to me. "Did I hear someone call you Gaby?" she asked, playing with her ponytail to turn it into a messy bun. She had some cool pink highlights under her jet black hair.

"That's me, the one and only," I replied, hitting a ballerina pose that made her giggle. "What's your name?"

"Marisa," she answered. She pointed to her head and did an exaggerated twirl in response. "It's my first day here. My dance team coach wants us to take classes in our off time, so I signed up for a package here."

"Oh, cool!" I answered. "So your school has a dance team?"

"Not exactly," said Marisa, putting her right foot on the barré and leaning over to touch it with her hand. "I'm on an all-star team."

I couldn't hide my confusion. "Aren't all-star teams for cheerleaders?" I asked her. I, of course, knew all about the competitive cheer teams that were independent from schools or sports teams. But dance all-star teams? Never heard of them.

"Well, yeah, there's a cheer team at my gym, too," said Marisa, shrugging like it was no big deal. "But all-star dance teams are becoming really popular. We go to competitions and train just like the cheerleaders."

"No way!" I said, squatting into a *plié*. It sounded so cool. "Believe it or not, I'm actually a cheerleader. Just for Greenview Middle School, not an all-star team. What gym do you go to?"

"It's called Energy Xtreme," said Marisa. "Have you ever heard of it?"

I hadn't. But before I could ask more, our teacher, Olivia, walked into the room. She clapped her hands to quiet everyone down. I gave Marisa an apologetic look and mouthed, "Let's talk later." I knew Olivia would flip out if we were whispering. It may have been a rock-and-roll ballet class, but it was still ballet!

"Okay, is everyone fully stretched?" asked Olivia. As we all nodded, she turned on some warm-up music. It was time to start across-the-floor exercises. "Everyone get in lines of three. We'll begin with *chaîné* turns," she instructed.

An old Eurythmics song filled the room. I loved this class because it had the upbeat feel of a jazz or hip-hop class, but it allowed us to practice our ballet moves. To me, basic ballet was kind of a snoozefest, but I couldn't deny that knowing the fundamentals definitely made me a better all-around dancer — and cheerleader!

"Don't forget to spot, Gaby," called Olivia as I took my turn across the floor. I often got dizzy during turns. Spotting was an art in itself! I had a hard time keeping focused on a single spot while I made my spins.

Marisa took her turn a few lines after mine. I watched in awe. She was really, really good.

We continued going back and forth, practicing *jetés*, *pas de bourrés*, and some other moves. Marisa continued to impress me with her elegant, powerful form. The class flew by. At the end, I noticed my friend Brooke watching through the observation window. We were supposed to grab some lunch, so I guess she'd come early to check out my class.

"Who's that?" asked Marisa, coming up behind me as I packed my dance bag.

"Oh, that's my friend Brooke," I said with a smile. "We're co-captains of our cheer squad. We're going to get some grub — this class always makes me so hungry! Our plan is to try this new vegan place a few doors down."

"I've been there — it's delish," said Marisa. She seemed so hip; I should have realized she'd already know about anything new and cool. "Are you vegetarian?"

I laughed. "Not even a *little* bit!" I said. "I'm obsessed with all kinds of food, especially candy and desserts. Brooke's the health nut, but I agreed to go because they supposedly have to-die-for cashew cheese fries and carob-chip smoothies. Do you wanna join us?"

"Man, I *so* would, but I actually have practice," said Marisa, slinging her ballet shoes over her shoulder. "Hey, you should come check it out sometime. Lots of the girls have cheer backgrounds, and I bet our coach would love to meet you."

How fun would that be? I thought. "Mos def!" Then I saw Brooke, standing in the hallway with her arms crossed. She was pretty punctual, so she didn't like to wait around for anyone else. It was a miracle that she still hung out with me, since I'm not exactly the princess of punctuality.

"I gotta jet, but here's my email and phone number," I said, scribbling it down on some scrap paper. "Send me all the info."

She tucked the piece of paper in her hoodie pocket. "Perfect-o," she said. "Hope to see you soon!"

When I met up with Brooke, she was full of questions. "Who was that?" she asked as we went out the studio doors. "I'm pretty sure Rainbow Brite called, and she wants her neon highlights back."

"Hey, they're cool!" I said in Marisa's defense, even though it *was* kind of funny. "She's actually a really good dancer. She's even on an all-star team. Besides, you're talking to the girl in a radioactive tutu."

"Good point," Brooke said, laughing. She gave my bright green tutu a little tug. "You two are birds of a style feather."

"Well, we might be birds of an all-star feather pretty soon," I told her. "She invited me to come check out a practice at her gym."

Brooke stopped in her tracks. "I hope that's a joke! Our plates are already fuller than a Vegas buffet," she said. "Coach Adkins would not be happy. You know she expects us to make the squad our first priority, especially as co-captains."

"Sloooow down, sista," I said. "No need to press the panic button! I'm just going to go see what it's all about — that's all."

"All right," said Brooke slowly. She didn't look convinced. I wasn't too worried about it, though. Brooke liked to do things by the book, but she'd come around when she saw that I could easily do both. And to me, that sounded like a pretty fun prospect! Gaby Fuller, all-star dancer . . . ready to shine!

TEAM CHEER!
The best thing about middle school!

FIND OUT MORE ABOUT OUR TEAM

Plus, download fun stuff for you and your friends!

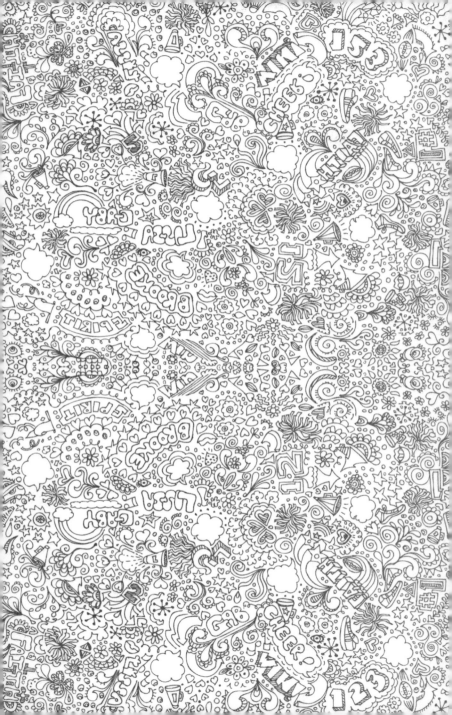

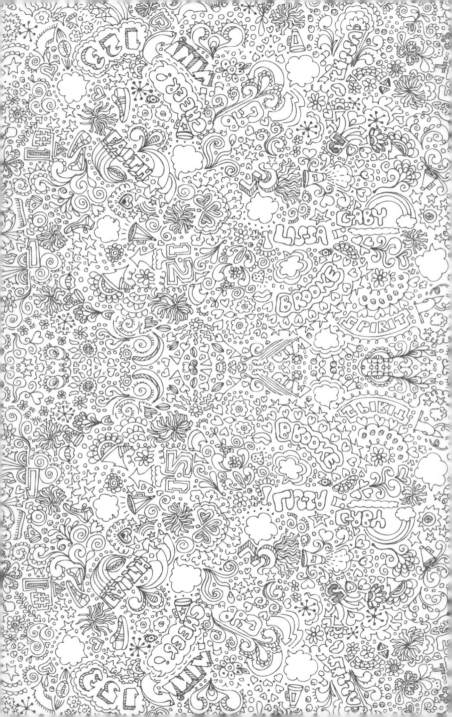

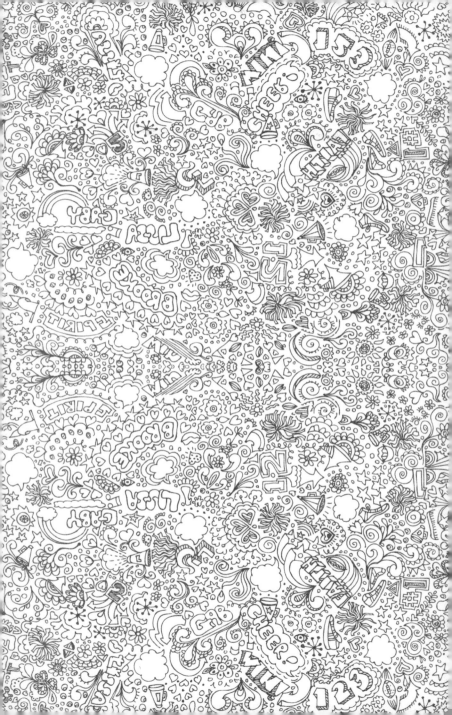

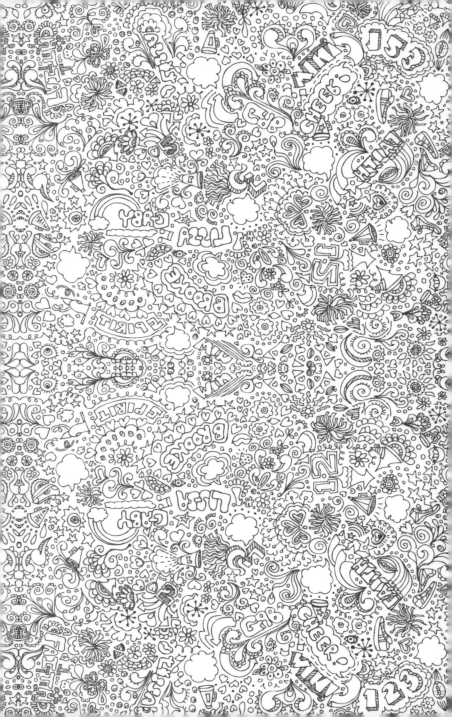